THREE

"Don't be rid very student at Fiel 's a sin to so much velt. We're above all

"Mick Farris isn't just any student from Roosevelt. He's co-captain of the squad. And you're a Falcon cheerleader. Everyone will think you're a spy or something."

"A spy! That's absurd! I couldn't tell Mick secrets about the football plays if I wanted to. Thanks for all the support," I said sarcastically.

Carla sniffed, and I could see she was offended. "What do you want from me anyway? You want me to tell you I think the entire student body will be just thrilled that the new love of your life is their Public Enemy Number One? You know as well as I do that some people are going to say you're a traitor."

I tried to push back the anger boiling up inside me before I said something I'd be sorry for. After all, what Carla was saying was probably true. But it was so unfair!

CHEERS FOR LOVE

"...ridiculous, Carla," I said sharply. "Ev...
...est High School can't think th...
...as talk to someone from Roose...
...that."

Three Cheers For Love

Suzanne Rand

BANTAM BOOKS

TORONTO · NEW YORK · LONDON · SYDNEY · AUCKLAND

RL 6, IL age 11 and up

THREE CHEERS FOR LOVE
A Bantam Book / January 1985

Cover photo by Pat Hill

ISBN 0-553-24385-3

Published simultaneously in the United States and Canada

Printed and bound in Great Britain by Hunt Barnard Printing Ltd.

O   0 9 8 7 6 5 4 3 2 1

We're from Fieldcrest,
Gold and Tan,
The Falcons are the finest
In the land!
Come on, fellas,
Give it your all.
Make those mighty
Rattlers crawl!

Traditional cheer for
Fieldcrest High School Falcons
versus Roosevelt High School Rattlers

Chapter One

From the grandstand area back beyond the ivy-covered PE building, the Cheerleading Camps of America's staff's voices could be heard loud and clear:

We're from C.C.A.
And we love to cheer!
We're from C.C.A.
And we're glad
You're here!

I knew I should be over in the stands, where the rest of the campers were congregating, instead of sitting on a hard stone bench in the sorority quadrangle. But as I stared blankly at the shuttered windows in a row of closed-up sorority houses, I felt that I wasn't ready to join the others. Not yet. I wanted to snatch a few minutes alone, even though I'd groused about my lack of company for half the summer.

After all, I thought as I shifted position on the uncomfortable seat, it wasn't as if I had much to feel friendly about. Earlier that summer I'd been virtually abandoned by my boyfriend, and a lot of my friends had gone away, too, or were busy with boyfriends. And now at camp I found myself surrounded by a group of total strangers.

Actually, not all the kids were total strangers; I'd already recognized one girl as I first walked down the hallway of the girls' dorm.

Great luck, right? I mean, running into an old friend? No such luck for yours truly, Mandy Birch. You see, the girl I'd recognized was Joy Moran. She'd been on the junior varsity cheering squad at Harrisville High School the year before, and anytime Fieldcrest's junior varsity teams had played against her school's, she'd given us all a royal pain. As my friend Carla said to me one time as we'd watched Joy bounce and flounce and do everything to get attention but elbow her fellow cheerleaders out of the way, "I suppose they named her Joy because it's such a joy when she leaves you alone."

If she was the one person I knew at camp, I'd just as soon be friendless.

I should have been happy. After all, just being at cheerleading camp was a real honor. You see, when school had ended in May, I'd been one of only two kids from the J.V. squad who'd made it through the competitions for the varsity squad, and out of the entire varsity squad for the coming year—seven girls and seven guys—I'd been chosen to receive this scholarship to camp.

So why, I asked myself as I stalled off the unavoidable moment when I'd have to join the others, was I feeling so glum? Partly because of the clothes I was wearing. I'd taken it for granted that we'd all be wearing the uniforms from our individual schools. I really loved my new varsity costume, with its short, flared skirt of deep gold and the tan knit top. I never imagined it would be practically snatched out of my hand the minute I arrived at camp. "We'll keep that for you until the final competition," a cheerful counselor had chirped when I was registering, and before I could even protest, the dry cleaner's bag was out of my hands and in a closet with a bunch of other uniforms from schools all over the East Coast. In return, the counselor handed me a pair of red gym shorts and a polo shirt with the C.C.A. logo splashed across it in white. I was told to unpack, change into the camp outfit, and meet the other kids out by the bleachers in two hours.

So sitting alone on the stone bench, I didn't feel like one of the stars of the Fieldcrest varsity

3

cheering squad anymore. Instead, I felt anonymous, Miss Anybody, dressed exactly like all the other kids at the small teachers' college where camp was being held.

I sort of felt like a little kid on her first day of kindergarten. After all, I'd spent my whole sixteen years—except for family vacations—in Fieldcrest. Now I'd been sent off—well, not exactly sent, since my mom and dad had made the three-hour drive with me—to some strange college in the middle of nowhere. And, I'd soon realized that at camp there was nothing special about me the way there was back home. I mean, all the kids were cheerleaders at their own schools. All of them were popular. And from what I'd seen of the girls so far, a lot of them were far prettier than I was.

Suddenly I was distracted from my thoughts by a voice.

"Why, Mandy Birch, it *is* you!"

Great! Joy Moran was rushing toward me. Her approach was enough to make me bounce to my feet, suddenly eager to be surrounded by all those strangers.

"Hello, Joy," I greeted her, trying to force a warmth I didn't feel into my voice. From the look in her green eyes as they fastened on mine, I could tell I'd failed.

Not that she'd ever go so far as to reveal her true feelings. Oh, no, not Joy.

"It certainly is a small world, isn't it?" she murmured as we started walking toward the stands. Sweetly she added, "I'd heard you'd won Fieldcrest's scholarship, but I told everyone there was no way Mandy Birch was going to leave that cute boyfriend of hers on the loose for a whole week. How is Danny, anyway?"

Joy's innocent tone didn't fool me for a second. I knew darned well she knew what was going on.

"Oh, didn't you hear?" I asked brightly, determined not to let her see she'd touched a sore spot. "Danny's gone. His dad was transferred to a bank in Saudi Arabia. They left right after school was out."

"Oh, Mandy, what a shame! How awful for you to be deserted like that!" Joy sounded about as sincere as the dentist when he says it won't hurt. "I'm surprised Danny didn't work out some way to finish school at Fieldcrest so he could be close to you."

Just about the whole world knew how downright *thrilled* Danny had been at the prospect of living in a foreign country, and I sensed that Joy was no exception. I didn't figure it was worth my while to lie about something she seemed to know the painful truth about, so as offhandedly as I

5

could, I just said, "Oh, he'd have been crazy to pass up a chance to travel. And after all, I was excited about going to Europe next Christmas, even before I knew Danny wouldn't be around, so how could I blame him for feeling the same way? You *did* know my parents and my sister and I are flying over to visit my brother, didn't you?" I added smugly, knowing very well Joy had never been anyplace exciting in her whole life. "He's stationed in Germany with the army."

"How terrific," Joy said in a voice that suggested it was anything but. Still, my remark had served its purpose. Now that she couldn't needle me, she shut up, and we walked the rest of the way to the bleachers in a welcome silence.

Oddly enough, I almost regretted having snubbed Joy when we reached the grandstand area and she immediately ditched me to sit with some girl she'd just met, leaving me looking alone and friendless. Smiling with lots more confidence than I felt, I found a place on a bench between two girls who didn't seem to know each other and who looked about as lonely as I felt.

To think that just a few days earlier I'd been thrilled at the prospect of getting out of Fieldcrest for a whole week! I'd seen cheerleading camp as an escape from a dreary, Dannyless summer. It was bad enough missing him, but the summer was turning out to be a drag in other ways as well.

For one thing, my brother, Terry, who'd graduated the year before, had been overseas for six months. For the first time I had a summer without his rushing in and out of the house, having a million things going on at once. If I was bored he would usually let me tag along with him.

And, because we were all flying to Europe in December, the family wasn't taking a summer vacation at all. That didn't raise my spirits any.

Then there was my younger sister, Joanna. She had turned fourteen in June, and she'd also turned impossible, practically overnight. That summer Jo had her first real boyfriend, this twerpy kid from her class named Reid who'd recently decided he wanted to be a rock star and had changed his first name to Real. Like most of my friends, Jo was now all tied up in her own romance and had no time for me. And, like her beloved Real, Jo had found a new name of her own. She wanted to be called by her full name, but she insisted on its being pronounced Jo-aw-na, and she all but snapped my head off when I forgot to pronounce it right—which is to say, wrong.

So you can see why I jumped at the chance to get away to camp. Still, I thought dismally as I watched the staff coaches execute complicated jumps I couldn't imagine myself doing in a million years, I'd had no idea it would be like this. I'd pictured myself surrounded by new friends, not tongue-tied in a group of people who might all be like Joy Moran.

And it had never even occurred to me that all the boys attending this coed camp would keep to themselves. Sure, I'd realized they'd have their own dorm and everything. But I'd never have guessed they'd all sit in a group at one end of the bleachers while we girls clustered at the opposite end.

No, I'd pictured guy after guy flirting with me while I basked in the center of attention. All summer long I'd caught myself wondering if there was something wrong with me—why else would a good-looking guy like Danny go off to the other side of the world without giving a thought to leaving me behind?

Sitting in the bleachers, I was certain there was something wrong with me. Forgetting about the gymnastics going on in front of me, I turned to check out the half of the bleachers that might have been labeled For Men Only. Most of the guys were sprawled this way and that, joking together and acting as interested in us girls as they would have been in the plague.

But just as I was giving up all hope, I focused on someone staring straight at me. Suddenly I felt terribly flustered, as if he could read my mind and knew that I thought this whole camp thing was turning out to be a drag.

Then he grinned, and his tanned, handsome face lit up as he ran his fingers through a thatch of thick, sun-bleached blond hair. Before I even felt my mouth moving, it had curved into a smile, and I was grinning back as if we shared the most wonderful private joke in the world.

Flustered again, I looked away, and desperate not to look pathetic in case he was still watching me, I turned to the dark-haired girl seated to my right. "Aren't they terrific?" I remarked brightly, gesturing toward the cheerleaders below us. "I'd give anything to be able to jump like that."

"Oh, me, too!" she agreed quickly, her voice loud and as bright as mine. I got my second surprise since I'd sat down when she said, her voice thick with emotion, "Boy, am I glad you sat next to me! My name's Sally Harris, and I didn't think anybody here was ever going to say a word to me for the entire week!"

In spite of my own nervousness, I laughed. "My name's Mandy Birch, and I sort of felt the same way. I guess maybe we're all so nervous, we were waiting for someone else to say something first."

"You're not kidding!" This time it was the girl on my other side, a tall skinny girl with a Bo

Derek braided hairdo that didn't look at all dated on *her*. "I'm Donelle Magee, and I'd just decided if someone didn't break the ice soon, I'd have to do it myself. Not that I meant to listen in or anything," she added apologetically.

Well, all three of us laughed at that, and before long we were chattering away as if we'd known each other since nursery school. And when the cheering coaches asked us to stand up and join them in the C.C.A. cheer, I was on my feet as fast as everybody else. Just before we all started clapping out the rhythm of the cheer, I let my eyes slide sideways until they rested on the blond guy again. You know what? He was looking back at me. And not only did he smile this time, he winked at me, too!

I might have a good time after all, I told myself as I flashed a big smile his way. Then, I turned back toward the lively group on the field and started clapping till my hands hurt.

Chapter Two

Before I get too caught up in telling what happened to me that fateful week, I guess I should explain a little bit about what cheerleading camps are. Some schools send their entire squads to camp; some are camps for girls only; some last all summer long; some are strictly for pom-pom squads. Like the one I attended, most of them are held on college campuses.

The brochure I'd been sent by Cheerleading Camps of America had explained that we'd be coached in learning new cheers, partner stunts, pom-pom routines, jumps, song routines, and sideline cheers. There would also be discussions on organizing and leading pep rallies and promoting school spirit. Cheering competitions held on the last day of camp would be the high point of the week, but no day would go by without some camp members being singled out for enthusiasm, talent, or spirit.

By the time the leaders had finished up that introductory cheering session the first day, the change in our own spirit was amazing. When I'd first approached the bleachers with Joy, most of the kids had looked listless, almost bored. But as the coaches led us in a final welcoming cheer, all our voices were raised in excitement and anticipation. The change in the kids' attitude made me realize that everybody else must have felt as alone as I had. After all, most of these kids came from towns scattered all over the East and probably didn't know more than one or two people at camp, if any; it was only natural we'd all feel a little out of it at first.

When the cheering stopped and we'd all quieted down, one of the staff members, a bouncy little thing with shaggy, strawberry-blond hair who looked younger than most of the campers, stepped forward and picked up a megaphone. With a smile brighter than the sun overhead, she shouted, "Hi, everybody, and welcome to the best week of your lives!"

By now, excitement was running high, and she had to wait until all the whistles and applause died down before she could continue. "My name's Midge Bevans—and, by the way, Midge is short for Margaret, not midget." We all laughed at that, then cheered when she added,

"I'm four foot eleven and proud of every inch of it!

"I'm also a cheerleader back home in Indiana, where I'll be starting my junior year in college come fall. All of us here"—she gestured with one hand to include the others lined up with her on the playing field—"are college cheerleaders who've been specially trained to lead the C.C.A. camps. Our goal is to teach you so much in seven short days—and to show you such a fantastic time—that you'll never forget us!"

She introduced the rest of the staff then, each of whom executed a perfect split or high jump in turn. "Now, we want to meet you and make sure you all meet each other! There are close to a hundred of you for this camp term, and we want you all to be acquainted by tomorrow when we'll start working you till you beg for mercy. So let's all go to the cafeteria in the main building for snacks and name tags and a get-acquainted hour."

By then I was eager to meet the rest of the kids—especially the cute boy with sun-streaked, golden hair. I saw him ahead of us as I walked toward the main building with Sally and Donelle. He was ambling along with two other guys, and they seemed lost in conversation. It was difficult to fight the temptation to rush ahead and introduce myself, but I knew I shouldn't act too forward with a boy I didn't know.

As I realized what I'd just been thinking, I had to bite my lip to keep from laughing at myself. Less than an hour earlier, I'd been moping around telling myself how miserable I was with Danny gone, and now there I was, daydreaming about a stranger! I really couldn't help it, though. I hadn't so much as looked at another boy since I'd first started dating Danny, but this blond kid was different. I knew he was.

For one thing, I had a funny feeling I knew him from someplace. There was something just vaguely familiar about him. But maybe it was just that as our eyes met, the chemistry I'd felt had been so strong it just seemed as if he were someone I recognized. I couldn't figure it out. I just knew that I had to meet him—for the first time or again, whichever it was—and the sooner the better.

I didn't get my chance right away, though. It turned out that Sally was the kind of girl who didn't do *anything* fast. She had a slow, lazy way of talking most of the time, and her pace at everything else matched her speech. So, by the time we reached the cafeteria, Sally and Donelle and I were pretty well acquainted, but there wasn't a single seat left at the table where you-know-who sat with some other guys.

Of course, since there weren't any girls at that table, I wouldn't have had the nerve to plop myself down there anyhow. I've never been the brazen type. So it was probably just as well that, after we'd gotten our name tags from the staff members sitting at a table by the entrance, the three of us made our way over to the only half-filled table in the room. I was happy to see Joy Moran wasn't among the kids already seated there.

Midge casually called us to attention, then asked us to stand one at a time, introduce ourselves, and tell the group where we were from. Our table was one of the first, and I felt shy and tongue-tied when my turn came.

I raised myself on stiff legs, placed my damp palms flat down on the cool Formica tabletop for support, then, taking a deep breath and keeping my eyes fixed firmly on Midge and the other cheerleading coaches, concentrated on not mumbling or stammering as I said, "My name is Mandy Birch, and I'm from Fieldcrest, Connecticut, which is a suburb of New Haven. I'll be a junior in the fall and on the varsity squad at Fieldcrest High. I was on the J.V. squad for the past two years."

I sank back down again as Donelle stood to speak her piece. I was glad my turn was over, not just because I've never liked having to address big groups of people—I love cheering, but having to speak by myself is different—but because every fresh introduction brought me closer to finding out the blond guy's name.

As it turned out, his introduction was all but unnecessary. You see, just as his turn came, it hit me who he was. It was just that I hadn't recognized him right away in the new surroundings.

"Hi, there," he said in a soft, deep voice that sounded cool and confident. "My name is Mick Farris. I live in New Haven, and this fall I'll be a senior and the co-captain of the Roosevelt High School cheering squad."

He flashed a smile my way as he took his seat again, and this time there was nothing—not even shyness—to keep me from smiling back warmly. After all, it wasn't as if we were total strangers. Besides, I thought, it was only good sportsmanship to go out of my way to be friendly to a rival.

Yes, Mick Farris was a rival, all right. And back home he was practically a legend. You see, two years earlier Mick had been the star of Roosevelt High's junior varsity football team—until he'd hurt his neck in a scrimmage. His doctor had told him to give up rough sports, and rather than let his athletic talent go to waste, Mick joined the Roosevelt cheering squad. He was also on the student council and in the honor society—an all-around, school-spirited type.

It didn't surprise me that I hadn't been able to place him at first. After all, I'd been cheering against Roosevelt's J.V. squad the year before and not the varsity. Also, as far as I could remember, I'd only seen Mick at a few games in the fall and winter. And his hair had been a deeper color then, not lightened by the sun to the color of butterscotch. I was sure it had been longer as well. My stomach did a bunch of crazy flip-flops as it hit me that I'd be seeing plenty of Mick in the year to come. You see, Roosevelt and Fieldcrest had played against each other in every team sport for as long as anybody could remember. I mean, when my dad had been a high-school football player, he'd played on the Fieldcrest team that had grabbed the division title from Roosevelt for the first time in six years, and he *still* talks about it.

The Roosevelt Rattlers and the Fieldcrest Falcons almost invariably placed number one and number two in our conference in every sport—except track and field events, and neither of our schools excelled there. Every year, either in football, basketball, baseball, or tennis, the contest for a division championship would usually mean a neck-and-neck battle between the Rattlers and the Falcons. The rivalry was so intense that last year when we'd read *Romeo and Juliet* in English class, our teacher, Ms. Pratt, had compared the Montagues and the Capulets to Roosevelt and Fieldcrest. And there was Mick Farris, the star of the Roosevelt cheering squad, smiling at me as if we'd been best friends forever.

He wasn't even just smiling anymore. The introductions were over, and the staff had suggested we all mingle and get acquainted while we enjoyed the punch and cookies they'd be serving. Mick was already on his feet, and he seemed to be heading my way.

Remember to play it cool, I warned myself. *Don't gush and make a big fuss over him like everyone else does.*

And then he was there, looking down at me, his eyes sparkling in amusement. "I know I'm supposed to be the enemy, but I figure here at camp it's good sportsmanship and not school rivalries that count," he said easily. "And I figure Mandy Birch has got to be Terry Birch's sister, right? I used to love to watch him play basketball."

I couldn't find my voice—it seemed to have fallen asleep someplace around the base of my throat—so all I could do was sit there with a silly grin on my face. It didn't seem to faze Mick, though. He just settled himself into the chair that Donelle had left empty as comfortably as if we were sitting in his living room. "See," he went on, "I used to be a real athlete. But that—"

Abruptly my voice returned. "I know. That was before you got hurt and became a cheerleader instead. I can't believe I didn't recognize you! Mick Farris! You're a real celebrity back in Connecticut. You're . . ."

My voice just sort of petered out as my ears became aware of what my lips were saying, and I felt my face go red with embarrassment. Why, I'd been gushing like a silly kid! So much for keeping my cool.

But instead of looking at me as if I were some kind of moron, Mick laughed lightly as he reached over and squeezed my hand. "You mean you're willing to forget we're fierce fightin' foes for the rest of the week? Whew! Am I glad to hear that! It really took all my nerve to come over here," he confessed.

"It took all *your* nerve to talk to *me*?" I murmured weakly.

He nodded. "Sure. What if you'd said, 'Get lost, you Roosevelt creep'? I wouldn't have known what to do, especially since I've been dying to talk to you since I first saw you out on the bleachers."

"You have?"

"I sure have." He paused for a second, then,

with a little shrug, he said earnestly, "I probably shouldn't be coming on so strong so soon, but, you see, I believe in chemistry more than I believe in rivalry."

"Me, too," I whispered. Then I broke out in a fit of giggles. I just couldn't help it. "I was going to say we should shake hands and be friends," I finally explained, seeing the puzzled look on Mick's face. "But you're already holding my hand."

Mick looked down in astonishment when he realized he'd never let go of my hand. Then, squeezing my hand even tighter, he started to laugh himself. And I think at that very instant I knew I was in love.

Chapter Three

Meeting Mick was like a dream come true. It wasn't only the best thing that had happened to me since school let out, it was the best thing *ever*. I look back on that week at cheerleader camp as the happiest seven days I can remember, and I've got to use all my powers of recollection to recall how grouchy and downhearted I was for those first couple of hours.

From the start I had a hard time believing it was all really happening to me. I mean, one of the neatest boys in the whole state of Connecticut interested in Mandy Birch and making no "buts" about it? That was like something out of the movies.

I guess the only thing that made me accept it was Mick's obvious sincerity. From the moment our eyes first met, I knew that he was someone who didn't play games with people and who wouldn't be able to put on an act if he tried. I also couldn't help feeling that I deserved something wonderful after all that had happened and that that something wonderful was Mick.

Have you ever felt that way? First there was Danny leaving, going happily off to his exciting new life and not worrying one bit about leaving me. Then there was missing my brother so much, my sister's turning into the Bride of Frankenstein, and my family's decision not to take a summer vacation.

And, on top of all this, there was my part-time summer job—which, unfortunately, I was going to have to go back to once camp was over. I'd been pretty pleased at being hired by Benson's Department Store, imagining myself talking with shoppers at the counters and spending my afternoons in the busy hubbub of the first-floor cosmetics department or the second-floor juniors sportswear department. If I'd paid more attention at the job interview, I guess I wouldn't have been in for such a letdown when I'd shown up on my first day and been led straight back to a dingy stockroom.

"Oh, we start all our new employees in inventory," the personnel manager explained when she saw the way my face had fallen. "It's only those who show dedication and enthusiasm who are eventually moved on to positions on the sales floors. Everyone starts right here in the stockroom." She sounded sympathetic, and I suspected she'd started there herself and had liked it just about as much as I expected to.

So, you see, by the time I'd arrived at cheer-leading camp, I'd collected more than enough reasons for feeling a bit sorry for myself. That's why it seemed that Mick had been sent my way to even the score.

He more than evened it. He sent it positively soaring from the minus column to the plus column. From the moment Mick came over to me in the cafeteria that first day, we were together. Neither of us really questioned our being drawn to each other the way we were. It just seemed so right and so natural, we more or less took it for granted.

I don't mean to suggest I dumped all my other newfound friends to spend time with Mick. I really liked Donelle and Sally, and I wanted to get to know them better, too. And as it turned out, I didn't even have to consider ignoring them, or my new roommates, Candy and Tina, for Mick. The boys at C.C.A. followed Mick's lead when he ambled across the cafeteria to talk to me. Within fifteen or twenty minutes, it was no longer boys in one place and girls in another. Instead, every-one was mingling, boys and girls together, and that's how we stayed for the rest of the week.

Actually Mick and I didn't get much of a

chance to talk to each other that first day. Just minutes after he'd first sat down next to me, we were surrounded by other kids. It seemed as if everyone was talking at once. A stranger walking into that lunchroom would never have guessed that just an hour earlier we'd all been sitting around like stones. But once our tensions eased, we all talked like crazy.

"Oh, *definitely*!" I assured a bunch of girls who came over to ask if I preferred cheering for football. "That's when you can do the best cheers. Basketball cheers aren't bad, either."

"We have to cheer for just about everything," a little redhead groaned, wrinkling her freckled nose. "Do you know what it's like to cheer for a wrestling match? *Boring*!"

"But I like to cheer at wrestling," Sally Harris drawled. "There's not as much for the fans to watch, so they can pay more attention to *me*."

"Yeah, but how many times can you chant, 'Pin him down, on the ground'?" asked a guy whose name tag said Todd. "That can't begin to compare with 'Push 'em back, shove 'em back, waaay back!' "

"If that's your best football cheer," Mick remarked with a twinkle in his gray eyes, "your school must not be the local champs."

We all chuckled at that, and I felt this funny little glow of pride at Mick's clever remark—almost as if he were already my boyfriend. Still I have to confess I was sort of relieved when the other kids had joined us. It was all happening so fast my head was spinning, and I didn't quite know how to act toward Mick. So it was just as well we weren't alone. On one hand, I felt as if we had some sort of understanding, a closeness. On the other hand, I didn't really know Mick all that well. Practically everything I did know about him was hearsay and gossip. Being with him in the middle of a group of other people would give me a chance to get to see what he was really like without romance getting in the way.

We almost didn't get to the romance part at all. As soon as we'd had our snacks, Midge—who seemed to be the spokesperson for the staff—told us we were all going to the gym for some calisthenics and warm-up exercises, then back outside in smaller groups to practice high kicks, mule kicks, and split jumps.

The exercise bit was too demanding for me to keep an eye on Mick, and when we got outdoors, he was put into one group, and I was in another. I noticed that Joy Moran was in the same group as he was, and a little twinge of envy nipped at me. Even though Joy liked to hog the limelight, there was no denying that she was a super gymnast and an excellent cheerleader. I didn't want Mick to compare my talents to Joy's and rank me in second place. But I knew I was silly to worry. At this camp there were scores of kids who could jump better than I could, not to mention girls who were really gorgeous. In spite of all that, I'd been the one whose "chemistry" had attracted Mick, so why should I worry?

Besides, I'd started having too much fun to waste time with jealousy. Our group of ten was being coached by a girl named June, who appeared plain and withdrawn until she opened her mouth. Then she sparkled with enthusiasm, her dark eyes flashing and her sallow skin turning rosy. I liked her a lot immediately, maybe because she reminded me of myself.

You see, cheerleading had really turned me into a new person. Up until the summer before ninth grade, I'd been one of those girls who sat back and let other people shine. I guess it had something to do with being the middle child in my family. I'd always thought of my brother Terry as the closest thing to a Greek god because he was athletic and good-looking and always popular in school. Even to myself, I was Terry Birch's kid sister first and Mandy Birch second.

Jo hadn't been close enough in age to Terry to worry about measuring up to him when she started school. And since she was little and bouncy and dark like my mom instead of lean, lanky, and sandy-haired like Terry, me, and our dad, people didn't immediately spot her as Terry Birch's sister. So maybe it had been easier for her to be outgoing right from the start.

Anyhow, even though I knew the other kids in my class liked me, I never tried to be a leader or a school star or anything. I was content to stay in the background, even though lots of times I wished I could be special like my brother instead of just average.

It was Carla who'd pushed me. I'd always been surprised, ever since she'd picked me as her best friend back in grade school, that a girl who was so outgoing and lively and not afraid of a single thing would be so crazy about me. And that summer before ninth grade, she really lit into me. "You're never fair to yourself, Mandy," she insisted. "You always see yourself as second best, but nobody else does. Now, I'm planning to try out for the J.V. cheerleading squad before school starts, and you're going to practice and try out with me. No ifs, ands, or buts about it."

That's how Carla is when she feels strongly about something—like a steamroller. It didn't seem worth arguing with her, and anyway, practicing for the tryouts would give me something to do for the summer. I knew I'd be eliminated in the first mass competition, and then life would get back to normal.

But that's not the way it happened. One day at

the park, where we were practicing our jumps, this guy I knew slightly from school wandered over to watch Carla and me. It was Danny, and that's how I started going out with him.

For another, I discovered that cheering was becoming important to me. I'd always been proud of my school and its teams, and I longed for the chance to stir up even greater school spirit. And yelling and jumping made me come alive. You can't fade into the background when you're shouting and kicking in front of hundreds of other kids. Before we'd been practicing a week, I knew I wanted desperately to be a cheerleader; I wasn't just going along with Carla anymore. But I hoped I wouldn't be too crushed when I didn't even make it to the finals. After all, to be a Fieldcrest cheerleader you had to be *terrific*.

Well, to make a long story short, somehow I made it through the finals and onto the squad. And I finally started to believe what Carla had been trying to tell me all along: that I wasn't second best and I had no reason for not going after whatever I wanted.

That's why at camp I identified with June; I was sure she'd started out a lot like me. Cheering was clearly the thing that turned her on and gave her self-confidence. And even though she didn't jump as high as some of the other coaches, she had something special we all responded to. For two hours I worked so doggedly and got so caught up in what we were doing that I didn't even think about the other kids scattered around the playing field.

When Midge finally blew the whistle to stop, I was exhausted, and the other kids looked just as sweaty and tired. But as I looked around, I noticed everyone seemed pretty peaceful and happy in spite of their exhaustion.

"OK!" Midge boomed in her strong voice. "Everyone back to their respective dorms to wash up. We'll meet in the cafeteria in an hour and a half for a song session before dinner."

"Let's wait for Candy, Tina, and Donelle," I suggested to Sally, who'd been in my practice group, "so we can all walk back together." Of course, I was secretly hoping Mick would walk back with us, too, because the boys' dorm was next to ours.

It turned out that Mick was right on the heels of the three girls. But my heart sank when I saw that Joy was at his side, her blue eyes round with cowlike devotion. From the way she was talking a mile a minute, it was clear that she was putting the moves on him. Was Mick the type of guy who could be taken in by an act as obvious as hers?

I wondered. When they got close enough for

me to hear, Joy all but batted her eyelashes and murmured to him, "I'll see you in the cafeteria then."

Mick didn't even have a chance to say hello before two of the guys practically mowed us down. "Come on, Farris!" one of them shouted, grabbing Mick's elbow as he dashed by. "Race you to the dorm!"

With a crooked, apologetic smile that didn't single out any one of us in particular, Mick was gone.

Well, I knew that no guy like Mick would pass up an athletic challenge from a buddy, so I didn't take his running off as a slap in the face.

Unfortunately I also knew Joy well enough not to trust her as far as I could throw her. And from the smug smile that kept twitching on her lips as we walked back across the grass to the dorm, I had no doubt she was busily planning how to get her hooks into Mick.

Chapter Four

"Hey, what's with that Joy? Is she full of herself or what?" Donelle flopped down on the foot of my bed, the sudden movement making the beads on all her little braids click together. She and Sally—who, it turned out, were sharing a room with each other and another girl neither of them was crazy about—had just arrived at our room, smelling of soap and looking fresh and revived in new jeans and almost identical tank tops.

"You guys look like Mutt and Jeff in those outfits. Now, what can I wear to dinner?"

"Hey, don't change the subject," Donelle scolded. "You're the only one who seems to know about her—we want all the dirt. I know trouble when I see it, and that girl is it."

I shrugged, pulling a pair of wheat-colored jeans and a blue oxford-cloth shirt out of the closet I shared with Tina. "She just likes to make life difficult for everyone." I sighed. "She must have seen that Mick was interested in me and decided to cause some trouble."

"How come?" Sally looked puzzled. "Are you two enemies from way back or something?"

"Nope. We're not friends, either. Joy just makes trouble for no reason at all. Maybe she's bored."

It must have been clear I wasn't very hopeful about my future because Candy, who hadn't said much all day, piped up firmly, "Don't you worry, Mandy. Mick seems too sharp for her."

"Oh, he's crazy about you. I could tell," Sally chimed in.

In spite of feeling worried about whatever mischief Joy had worked on Mick, I had to smile. Considering how short a time I'd known these girls, they sure were being supportive. "Thanks, guys," I said. "With friends like you, how could I worry about a zero like her?"

"That's the spirit!" Donelle sounded like a true cheerleader as she slid off the bed and stretched, stifling a yawn. "What do you say we go get this sing-a-ling thing over with? I'm starving."

"Yeah, all that jumping around made me ravenous," Sally agreed. "You all ready? Tina? Candy? Mandy?"

"Please!" Donelle laughed as we went through the doorway. "Tina, Mandy, Candy, Donelle, and

Sally. No wonder we've got to sing before we eat. If we don't sound like an all-girls' quintet, who does?"

By this time we were all sort of punch-drunk from a combination of physical tiredness and the giddy relaxation that goes with a release of tension.

We arrived at the cafeteria entrance harmonizing on old Beatles' songs—when we could stop giggling long enough to sing, that is. The sight of two empty seats at the table where Mick was already seated made me feel even more lighthearted, and I led the way while the other girls followed behind.

Even the sight of Joy Moran threading her way over to the chair next to Mick didn't get me down. I'd have had no reason to worry anyway, because as soon as Mick spotted me he called, "Here, Mandy! I've saved you a seat!"

Need I make a point of the ripples of satisfaction that swept over me as I watched the smile fade from Joy's face? Her lips a thin line of displeasure, she turned on her heels, trying her best to appear as if she'd been heading for a different table all along.

I settled down next to Mick, with Sally on the other side of me; the other three girls found seats together at the next table. Soon all thoughts of Joy were forgotten as I basked in being near Mick.

The staff led us in singing old standbys and taught us some new fight songs, too. We'd be singing them again after dinner, Midge explained, when we'd meet in the parking lot at the front of the administration building for a lesson in building what she called a "bedazzling bonfire."

Mick's and my conversation during dinner was pretty general because we were surrounded by other kids who joined in the talk and because I was making a conscious effort not to leave out Sally. It wasn't until Mick and I were alone, taking the long way through the quad toward the parking lot, that I finally asked him the question that had been nagging at me for the past few hours.

"I know it's none of my business, but what was Joy Moran talking to you about earlier?" I tried to keep my voice casual. "I've never seen her look so serious."

"Oh, her!" he snorted. "She's not a friend of yours, is she, Mandy? 'Cause you sure don't need friends like her."

"I don't know if Joy's anybody's friend, even her own," I said honestly. "What happened?"

Even in the dim light of early evening, I could

34

see the blush that reddened his tan. "Oh, nothing really."

"Come on, tell me." I was surprised at my own boldness, but I really wanted to know.

Mick shrugged. "She didn't say anything, really." He paused. "Well, she did say she'd noticed you and I were hitting it off. And, uh, she *did* say that back home you and this guy named Danny have such a great understanding."

"A great understanding!" I sputtered, stopping dead in my tracks. "I don't suppose she bothered to add that he moved to Saudi Arabia and doesn't plan to come back!"

"Hey, relax!" Mick chuckled, shaking his head. "I don't want to open up a can of worms. And if it makes any difference, I didn't pay attention to her anyhow. I can tell you're not the kind of girl who'd let some guy think you were available if you weren't. Besides, it was pretty easy to figure out she was just trying to line up some guys while she's at camp. Or didn't you notice how quickly she attached herself to that hulk from New York at dinner?"

I shook my head. I'd been so thrilled when Mick had called me over and Joy had gone off in a huff that I'd forgotten all about her after that.

"Anyway, let's forget about her," Mick suggested. "She's got nothing to do with us."

We were just about to turn the corner at the edge of the big brick building that separated the parking lot from the campus itself when suddenly Mick stopped. Though we couldn't have been more than a hundred feet from where the kids were already congregating and we could hear their raised, excited voices, the group itself was out of our line of sight.

"There's just one more thing, Mandy," Mick said slowly.

I stopped again and looked up at him, feeling as if I could melt under the warmth of his eyes. I hoped the deepening twilight hid the pulse at the side of my throat. My blood was racing. "What is it?" I asked in barely a whisper.

"It's this guy Danny." Mick turned his head slightly, avoiding my gaze, and his voice was choked and bashful. "After talking so big, I feel like a real jerk for asking this, but you don't still feel anything for him, do you?"

"Oh, no," I whispered, not thinking he was a jerk at all. To tell the truth, I was touched and flattered that it mattered to him. "I was upset when I first found out he was moving, but I was more mad at him for being so excited about going away. His dad got a job transfer," I explained. "I don't know, I suppose if he ever moved back to town, I'd want to be friends. But that's all we were, really. Friends who were going out together. It wasn't like the world's greatest love story or anything, not like my knees went weak every time I saw him, not like—"

I had to bite my lip to keep the words from rushing out, to keep from babbling "like you and me." But that's what I was thinking, and my knees were feeling pretty weak with Mick standing just inches from me. His tousled blond hair looked so silky I longed to reach out and run my fingers through it. His breath was warm on my cheek when he turned back to face me.

A magic spell could have descended upon us, that's how quiet we were. The noise of the parking lot suddenly seemed miles away, drowned out by the echo of my own heartbeat thudding in my ears.

It was almost like being at the movies and watching two people up on the screen, two people who weren't us. In my mind's eye, I could see Mick's hand reaching down to my waist as my arms slowly rose to encircle his neck. Then his lips were on mine, warm and gentle, in the sweetest kiss ever.

Chapter Five

"You mean it, Mandy? You really mean it?" Carla was sitting cross-legged on the spare twin bed in my room back home, practically bouncing up and down with excitement. "Wow! That's even more terrific than my new perm." She fluffed up her freshly frizzed, shoulder-length hair—which had been straight as a board when we'd said goodbye a little more than a week ago—then threw herself backward on the bed.

"Well, it *was* nice," I admitted from where I was sprawled on my own bed.

"Nice?" With a little shriek, Carla sat up abruptly, tapping her fingers against one ear. "I must be hearing things: you didn't really just describe meeting the boy of your dreams and having him totally fall for you as just plain 'nice,' did you, Mandy?"

"OK, it was more than nice. It was wonderful.

I'm really happy. And if I'm not bubbling over, it's just because I'm still in shock."

That was true. What was also true—which I didn't say—was that I didn't want to gossip about Mick, whose name I hadn't revealed yet, even though I'd given Carla a rundown on how we'd met and how everything had clicked at cheerleading camp. I was crazy about him, that was for sure, and I didn't have any doubts that he felt the same way about me, but I knew Mick was even more private a person than I was, and I didn't feel like blurting out every detail of our romance. Besides, there was one important thing about Mick I didn't want to tell Carla—not just yet.

"Well, I think it's just heaven about you and—what did you say his name is?"

I stuttered. "M-Michael. His name's Michael."

"And he lives close enough that you'll still be able to see him? Oh, Mandy, it's just like one of those romances my mom's always reading. It's so perfect. I mean, meeting Mr. Right just when you were so down about Danny and everything."

"So, how've things been going for you and *your* Mr. Right?" I asked, eager to move on to a different subject. "You still dating Greg?"

"Yeah, more or less." Carla was fickle and a notorious flirt. In spite of being such a romantic, she never stayed with one boy for long because she'd get bored. Or maybe she felt that way *because* she was so romantic. No one ever seemed to live up to her ideal, so she lost interest quickly.

"Anybody interesting on the horizon?"

"Well, I wouldn't mind going out with Moose Snyder. He'd have to get a new nickname, though. I mean, how could any self-respecting female ever say, 'And this is my boyfriend, Moose'?" She laughed, then paused as if she was trying to decide whether or not to tell me something.

I knew Carla, and I knew if I didn't say a word, she'd come out with it. She wasn't shallow, but she wasn't the deep, silent type, either. Anything that was on her mind would be on her lips soon enough.

As usual, I'd guessed right. No more than a minute later she said, "Promise you won't tell if I tell you who I'm really crazy about?" Then, without waiting for an answer, she said, "Keith Watkins. Isn't that insane?"

"What's so insane about it?"

"Just that Keith is one of the most popular guys in school—and on the cheerleading squad. Why should he look twice at a has-been like me? If only I hadn't been so lazy and practiced harder! I can't bear the thought of not cheering at the games anymore!"

"Don't worry, Carla," I said soothingly. "There's always next year. Why, you're one of the best cheerleaders I know! You'll definitely make the squad again."

"I know, I know," she said, sounding discouraged. "It's just that I want to be on it *now*, and knowing I've only got myself to blame doesn't help. There's no excuse for blowing those cheers at tryouts the way I did. Oh, I'm so jealous of you I could die! Making the varsity squad, winning the scholarship, and snagging a new boyfriend! Some people have all the luck!"

The quick switch of Carla's mood from merriment to misery didn't surprise me. She was always like that. But in another minute or two, I knew she'd be her usual cheerful self again, overflowing with plans to get Keith Watkins's attention. Still, I couldn't help feeling bad for her. After all, I never would have become cheerleader if it hadn't been for Carla's encouragement. But as she herself admitted, she should have known better than to think she'd automatically be pushed up onto the varsity squad without preparing more for the tryouts.

"Oh, I forgot to tell you." Carla was already climbing out of the doldrums. "I ran into your sister and that weird boyfriend of hers at the movies one night. Is his name really Real?"

"Don't be silly. It's Reid. He became Real when he decided to become a rock star. I think it's just a phase he's going through. Remember how dumb we acted when we were their age?"

"I guess we *were* almost as bad." She grinned. "Remember when I became Carlotta?"

I nodded. "That was right after my Amanda phase."

"Your sister's too much, though. 'From now on, please call me Jo-ahhh-nah.' "

I couldn't help laughing. Carla had mimicked Jo's new, almost-British accent perfectly. "The funniest thing is that she forgets how she wants it pronounced half the time. And she doesn't get at all uptight when Real slips and calls her Jo. I just hope she gets over it before she gets to high school. I wouldn't want my kid sister to be the laughingstock of Fieldcrest High."

That's when Carla asked the question I'd been dreading since she had come over, the question I'd been waiting for someone to ask me ever since my dad had picked me up at the college and brought me home two days earlier.

"Speaking of high school," she said off-handedly, "where does your new guy go to school?"

I gulped. "Roosevelt."

That snapped her to attention. "Roosevelt? Roosevelt High School! You mean you had to travel hundreds of miles to fall in love with one of our biggest rivals? Wait'll the other kids hear about this!"

"Hey, come on, don't make a big thing out of it," I pleaded. "Just because the two schools are rivals doesn't mean we all have to take it seriously."

"Yeah, but plenty of kids do. You know what it's like between the Falcons and the Rattlers, Mandy. I just hope this Michael isn't involved in sports, because if he is—" she stopped in midsentence, her blue eyes round as Concord grapes. "Wait a minute—of course he's involved in sports. You met him at cheerleading camp." Her eyes narrowed. "What did you say his name was? His last name, I mean?"

"Farris," I croaked.

It didn't hit her at first. She sat there looking puzzled, murmuring, "Michael Farris, Michael Farris." Then she let out a whoop. "Why, you rat!" She was laughing. "You're talking about Mick Farris, aren't you? All this Michael garbage was just so I wouldn't know, right? Mick Farris! Mandy, he's absolutely adorable!"

"Isn't he?" I agreed readily, relieved to have my secret out. "And he's fabulous, too. Just wait, Carla. You'll like him a lot."

"I probably will, but I don't know about everyone else." She shook her head, sounding doubtful. "Some of the Falcons will probably suggest having you hung for associating with the enemy. You know how serious they are about the competition. They'll be horrified."

"Don't be ridiculous," I said sharply. I went on, hoping I sounded more confident than I felt. "We're all adults—or practically adults. And we're supposed to be good sports as well. Don't tell me every student at Fieldcrest High School thinks it's a sin to so much as talk to someone from Roosevelt. We're all above that."

"Ha! You're fooling yourself if you think Mick Farris is going to be greeted with open arms at Fieldcrest because he's your boyfriend. He's not just any student from Roosevelt, remember. He's co-captain of the Roosevelt squad. And you're a Falcon cheerleader. Everyone will think you're a spy or something."

"A spy! That's absurd! I couldn't tell Mick secrets about the football plays if I wanted to, and I'm not about to rush over to Roosevelt and show him any cheers we come up with. Besides, he doesn't need *our* cheers. Didn't I tell you he won the cheerleading competition at camp? He took first place over everyone there. You're exaggerating."

"I hope so. What about him? Doesn't he know you cheer for the Falcons?"

"Of course he does. Mick's not a baby. He can rise above our rooting for rival squads. It doesn't matter to either of us." My little speech rang with dignity. I might have been pleading for our lives in front of a judge and jury. But I knew it was important to give the right impression, and I didn't want Carla to get the idea I was worried that the other kids might get down on me for going out with Mick. I didn't even want to put the idea in anyone's head that I was some kind of traitor for carrying on with the opposition. But Carla's reaction *did* have me worried. I had a suspicion things weren't going to be easy.

"Maybe you're right." Carla still sounded doubtful. "I'm not freaked out by the whole thing. And if you want to date a boy from Roosevelt, why shouldn't you? Boy, if someone as neat as Mick Farris fell at my feet, I know I'd have a hard time ignoring him! You've just got to follow your heart, Mandy. Do what you believe, no matter what. And if some of the kids get upset about it and try to make things rough for you, well, I'm sure they'll get over it."

"Thanks," I said sarcastically. "You've made me feel lots better."

Carla sniffed, and I could see she was

offended. "What do you want from me, anyway? You want me to tell you I think the entire student body will be just thrilled that the new love of your life is Public Enemy Number One as far as they're concerned? Give me a break, huh? You know as well as I do that some people are going to say you're a traitor."

I felt a blind anger boiling up inside me, and I tried to push it back down before I said something I'd be sorry for. After all, what Carla was saying was probably true. And it wasn't her fault if other people decided I was a real rat. But it was unfair!

Before I had a chance to respond, a loud shriek of stereophonic feedback and heavy bass line amplification jolted me from my thoughts. Carla and I both jumped up at the same instant. She clapped her hands over her ears.

"What in the world is that?" she finally managed to shout over the din.

"Love's young dream!" I bellowed back. "Real and his friends like to come over and serenade Jo when Mom and Dad are both at work. Come on, let's go tell them to put a lid on it before one of the neighbors calls the cops."

As we thumped down the two flights of stairs to the basement I felt a surge of gratitude toward my kid sister's boyfriend that was even stronger than the painful pounding of my eardrums. Real's so-called "music" had rung out just in the nick of time, ending a conversation I was starting to wish had never begun.

Chapter Six

Those few weeks before the school term started were heaven, and it was easy for me to push away any worries about what was going to happen. Mick had bought his own car the year before, an old junker of a compact station wagon with stuffing coming out of the seats and an exhaust pipe fastened to the back bumper with picture-hanging wire. It wasn't much, but as he said, "It gets me where I want to go." It got him back and forth between his house and mine, and that was what mattered.

Mom and Dad both approved of Mick, who treated them pretty much like he'd treated everybody at camp—casually, but with an underlying respect. It was easy to see that my kid sister really liked him, too—when she explained the "proper" pronunciation of her name, she did it with a shy sweetness and, for once, scrapped the usual exasperated, long-suffering sighs.

There's always plenty to do in our area as summer draws to a close—local fairs, the beaches, an Italian street festival to which people come to stuff themselves with delicious food. Twice Mick picked me up at work, and we drove to New Haven so we could wander around the beautiful old buildings at Yale. Mick hoped to go to college there to study political science. By then I was back to my original intention of wanting to become a grade school teacher. I'd almost forgotten that just before Danny had taken off for Saudi Arabia, I'd sworn to become a diplomat so I, too, could travel to fascinating places.

Of course I met Mick's family when we were in New Haven. His folks were a lot older than mine, both with graying hair, but they lived in the same kind of house on the same kind of street as ours. Their two-story colonial was nice without being spectacular, more quaint than impressive.

But inside, all resemblance to our house ended. The Farrises had nine kids. Mick was the middle one. And even with two of his older sisters already married with families of their own, the house seemed ready to burst at the seams, filled with children, grandchildren, and assorted friends. It was easy to see why Mick was so relaxed, though. For all the people in the house, voices were rarely raised. If one of the preschool grandchildren knocked over a mug of milk or something, Mrs. Farris would just murmur "uh-oh" and amble out to the kitchen for some paper towels to wipe up the mess. Both she and Mr. Farris took everything in stride.

Maybe it would have been better if I'd gradually introduced Mick to my crowd at school, but I'd never been big on meeting trouble head-on, and in this case I tried to postpone any unpleasantness for as long as possible. Of course I told myself there was no reason to make a big thing out of Mick's going to Roosevelt, but deep down inside, I couldn't help feeling anxious. I tried to relax by eating chocolate-chip cookies *constantly*, then had to diet the last week of vacation so my new school clothes wouldn't be too tight.

I didn't even make an effort to have him meet Carla in spite of her saying she thought he sounded terrific. Those few weeks, I knew, would be the last we'd be just Mick and Mandy instead of two kids from competing schools, and I wanted to get the most out of each minute together.

As a matter of fact, Mick and I didn't even discuss the possibility that our relationship might be scandalous to our friends when they found out. I just figured that he was satisfied with the promise we had made to each other the last day of cheerleading camp that we'd never let the Rattlers and the Falcons come between us. Besides, we were still at that stage where most of our feelings were unspoken. Not that we had to put them into words; we both knew we had something special, and I was sure it was only a matter of time before I would be his steady girlfriend.

I didn't avoid my friends when I wasn't with Mick. However, I'd sworn Carla to secrecy—hinting what a shame it would be if Keith Watkins were to find out how hung up on him she was—and when I went out with my other friends, I said nothing other than that I was dating a boy I'd met that summer and was no longer upset over Danny's leaving.

None of them pressed me for details, and everyone seemed to be happy to hear I wasn't turning into an old maid. Now that I no longer resented my girlfriends for having boyfriends, I realized that my loneliness earlier in the summer had been my own fault. They'd never been too busy for *me*—I'd just been too busy sulking to bother with them. But once our relations were back to normal, I didn't want to blow it by letting them know too much about Mick, and I guess they didn't want to upset things by seeming to pry.

So, at the end of summer, I was trying to keep my two lives separate. There was my life with Mick, and there was my life with Carla, Elaine, Judy, and Bev. There were also lots of wonderful letters from the new friends I'd made at camp.

Classes at Roosevelt began the same day as classes at Fieldcrest, and Mick and I were both starting back to school with mixed emotions because it meant we wouldn't be able to see much of each other except on weekends. He'd already invited me to the Roosevelt Fall Mixer, which I looked forward to but also made me feel a little queasy. I'd noticed that Mick's friends were as invisible to me as mine were to him, which is to say that I hadn't met even one of them when I was in New Haven. I wondered if Mick was as apprehensive as I was. Was he worried that his classmates would come down on him for getting involved with a girl who cheered for the Falcons?

In spite of my worries, I was ready to go when Mom called up the stairs to wake me on the morning of the first day of school. "I'll be right down!" I called, jumping out of bed and sliding my feet into my favorite pair of old terry cloth scuffs. I grabbed a light cotton robe to throw on over my baby doll pajamas as I left my room and paused only to bang on Jo's closed door on my way to the bathroom.

"Time to get up, Miss Jo-aw-na," I trilled in my best imitation of a ladies' maid. "If you miss out on a shower, don't blame me." Mornings are always hectic in our house, so the rule is that Jo showers while I eat breakfast. Before I went downstairs, though, I splashed water on my face, brushed my teeth, and thumped once again on Jo's door.

Dad was already dressed and at the table in the dining room, sipping coffee and skimming the headlines of the morning paper. Mom, wrapped in a duster, with her freshly washed hair peeking from a towel coiled turban-style around her head, was in the kitchen, chopping up ham and tomatoes to add to her and Dad's scrambled eggs.

"Morning, Mandy." She half turned to greet me. "There's hot corn bread in the oven. Should I count you in on the eggs?"

"No, thanks. None for me." The yummy aroma of hot corn bread wafted out as I opened the oven door. "Mmmm—I think I'll fill up on this." I took two big slabs of it, then poured a tumblerful of orange juice from the pitcher on the sideboard. Mom was a fiend about unprocessed foods, and she squeezed our juice fresh each morning. With my plate in one hand and glass in the other, I hurried through the swinging doors back into the dining room, eager to slather the bread with butter while it was still hot.

First-day excitement must have lit Jo's fuse because she came downstairs, looking alert and well-scrubbed before I'd even finished my breakfast.

"Aren't you going to be warm in that, dear?" Mom asked, looking uncertainly at my sister's favorite new outfit—a minidress of bright green sweat shirt material with green and blue striped leg warmers to match. "It's still summer, you know. The weatherman predicted a high of eighty this afternoon."

"Oh, Mom, really!" Jo answered in that exasperated and exasperating way of hers. "This is a hundred-percent cotton. It breathes, so it's perfectly comfortable."

"You're the one who's got to wear it, darling." As Jo bent her head over her bowl of cereal, Dad looked up, caught Mom's eye, and winked. As I got up to take the dishes into the kitchen, I grinned at them both. We were all becoming old hands at dealing with my sister's stubbornness by now. And we all knew that she'd arrive home in the afternoon red in the face and dripping perspiration but still insisting she was "perfectly comfortable."

Back upstairs, I showered and washed my hair, blowing it dry bit by bit whenever I took a break from dressing or making up my face. I longed to wear my new cheerleading outfit, but that wasn't allowed until the first practice. I finally settled on a royal blue poplin jump suit and a taupe belt to match my woven leather flats. The jump suit wasn't new—I'd picked it up at a spring sale—but at least I was going to be comfortable all day, unlike my sister.

I was dressed and ready, with plenty of time to spare, so I took my book bag out on the front porch and sat on the wrought-iron settee while I waited for Carla. She lived just two blocks away and had to pass my house on the way to school, so we'd always walked together. We'd taken the same path for years because the grade school, junior high, and high school were all clustered together less than half a mile away.

Dad drove off in the station wagon first, having to travel all the way to New Haven where he's an executive in an insurance company. Then Mom took off in her own little secondhand car to head for the shopping mall beyond the school complex, where she manages a small gift and card shop, and Jo scrounged a ride. I guess she figured that in her winter outfit she was in danger of dropping over from heat stroke if she walked. Besides, the kid is lazy.

Finally I saw Carla striding toward me along the sidewalk. Carla's mom is pretty bossy, and she always makes a fuss the first day of school about Carla's dressing "properly." So, as usual, Carla wore a simple white blouse, a pleated skirt, and "sensible" shoes. She used to get uptight about it, but now she just shrugs it off. Experience has shown her that by the end of the first week, her mother loses interest in her clothes—or maybe just loses the strength to argue every day—and Carla is back to the casual clothes she prefers.

"Sorry, I'm late," she said a bit breathlessly as I met her at the foot of the walk. "You know how my mom is the first day."

"Why bother putting up a fight then?" I asked as we started walking in the direction of school, keeping our pace slow so Carla could catch her breath.

"I haven't got any choice." She shrugged. "If I gave in too easily, she'd never give up. Then I could end up wearing these yucky clothes for the rest of my life."

We talked about the usual back-to-school stuff as we walked along: what teachers we were excited about, which we dreaded, new kids we'd heard had transferred into the area over the summer, how fall was in the air already even though the weatherman promised a scorcher by lunchtime.

We were walking up the wide, curving stretch

of asphalt that led to the school buildings when Carla asked bluntly, "How much longer do you think you can keep it a secret about you and Mick?"

"I am *not* keeping it a secret," I lied, my voice rising in indignation that sprang chiefly from being forced to fib. "I just don't think my love life should be everybody's business. Besides—"

I cut off my words as Keith Watkins, tall and gangly yet oddly graceful, fell into step beside us. "Hey, Carla, Mandy! How was your summer?"

"Great," I said, while Carla chirped, "Terrific!" at the same time.

"How was yours?" Carla asked Keith, and I couldn't believe he didn't notice her eyes glazing over as she gazed up at him or the breathiness that made her sound like a bad Marilyn Monroe impersonation. But I suppose when you're as popular as Keith's always been, you take hero worship in stride.

"I had a terrific time," he said enthusiastically. "Spent two whole months working on my uncle's boat. And I found a sweetheart of a sixteen-footer someone's thinking of selling in the spring. If I can save enough working after school for my granddad, I stand a good chance of getting it. How'd you girls like to go sailing next summer?"

"Oooh!" Carla was practically squealing with

excitement. "That sounds wonderful!" Then, some of her usual coolness came back to her. "Of course," she drawled, "it's a little far in advance to be making a date."

Keith picked up on the flirtatiousness in her voice this time. "Maybe we can work something out before that," he said and grinned.

Carla didn't answer, and I knew she must have been knocked speechless at the promise of a date with Keith. To break the awkward silence that swept over her, I said to Keith, "I can hardly wait to show you all the new cheers and stuff I learned at cheerleading camp. There are a couple of group routines I think would really look fabulous, and I'm sure the squad could learn them in time."

"Yeah?" He tore his gaze away from Carla, and his eyes met mine, lighting up with interest. "Do you think we can master them in just three weeks, in time for the game with Roosevelt?"

"Oh, uh, sure. They're not at all hard. Boy, some of the coaches at camp were something else! So professional! They all cheer for different colleges, you know."

I'd hoped to turn the conversation away from Roosevelt, but my hopes were in vain. "Well, I'm really looking forward to showing up the Rattler squad this year," Keith said. "If we can make their cheerleaders look lame, it'll do a lot for the guys on the team. I know the Falcons can cream the Rattlers this year, really cream them!"

"Sure," I agreed weakly, ignoring the sidelong look Carla shot at me, a look that told me I hadn't sounded enthusiastic.

We'd reached the wide, short flight of stairs that led to the school doors, and Keith glanced at his watch and said, "I've got to run. I told Bart Corrigan I'd meet him by the gym lockers to give back the weights I borrowed from him." He held up the gym bag that had been weighing him down as we'd walked. In spite of the heavy load, he took the stairs two at a time, turning back toward us when he reached the top. "Hey Carla, how about going to Jackson's after school for a Coke?"

"You bet!" she answered. I knew it was all she could do to keep from whooping.

"Meet you by the sports showcase," Keith called down. Then he raised his clenched right fist. "Make those mighty Rattlers crawl!" he yelled.

It was the last line of our traditional cheer against Roosevelt, and all around us voices were raised to echo Keith's war whoop. All the kids arriving at the school building shook their fists and shouted like bloodthirsty Indians. Then Keith turned and disappeared inside the building.

"I notice *you* didn't join the cheer," Carla said sweetly.

"And I notice *you* sounded ready to go out and massacre the Rattlers singlehandedly," I snapped. "What are you trying to do, make points with Keith?"

"Don't be ridiculous, Mandy! Whether you like it or not, the Rattlers are the enemy, and everyone at Fieldcrest is going to be out to beat them. As usual," she added pointedly. "And if I were you, I wouldn't go around giving kids the idea that your heart's not in the contest anymore now that you've got a Rattler rooter for a boyfriend."

"Don't *you* be ridiculous. I'm the same person I've always been, and my loyalty will always be for Fieldcrest."

"Well, you'd better stop keeping it so quiet about you and Mick Farris then. If the rest of the kids find out from someone else, they're really going to think something's funny."

"Stop making such a big deal out of it, would you?" I pleaded as we pushed through the doors into a crowd of jostling kids, who all were talking at once. I stopped. "I'll bet you five dollars I don't take any garbage from anyone after I break the news."

"It's a bet."

We shook hands, then parted to go our separate ways to our homerooms. I was uncomfortable as it struck me that I was more annoyed with Carla than I'd been in a long time. And I couldn't shake off the suspicion that I was going to be five dollars poorer very soon.

Chapter Seven

I found out the hard way that Carla was right.

Looking back, I wish I'd taken her advice and told everyone about Mick and me right from the start. Maybe if I'd been more up front about our relationship, things wouldn't have turned into such a mess. But I suppose it's foolish to get upset over how things might have been. Truth is that I was too cowardly to do what should have been the simplest thing in the world: to announce to my friends that I had a new boyfriend and that I was mad about him.

Tomorrow, was what I told myself every day. *Tomorrow I'll start telling people about Mick.* And the more I told myself tomorrow, the more I felt uncomfortable being around Carla. The slightest glance from her seemed to hold the unspoken accusation that I was weak-willed and two-faced.

If only I'd forced myself to think about the subject, I might have realized that the truth was going to sound a lot worse coming from someone other than me. But I didn't face up to that until it was too late.

Our first cheerleading practice was scheduled for fifth period the Friday after school began. At Fieldcrest, cheerleaders, like band and orchestra members, are allowed to use two study-hall periods a week for practice. Fourth period had just ended, and the fifth period bell hadn't rung yet. All of us cheerleaders were assembled in front of the double doors that led into the gymnasium where practice would be held.

Because this was a practice day, we were all wearing our uniforms. As usual, our pride in them made us linger in the hall to show them off to the other kids as they passed by. Thinking back, I can't even remember what anyone was saying or doing at the time. I do know I was standing with Keith Watkins, Will Hendricks, and April Adams, who was captain of the squad. They'd all been eager for me to show them some of the cheers I'd learned at camp. I was feeling happy and proud—little did I know that disaster was about to strike.

The first bell jangled, and the halls started clearing because the second—and late—bell would go off in just three minutes. We weren't in a rush, though; all we had to do to be on time was push through the doors and enter the gym.

A slender girl with sleek, dark hair was sort of wafting down the hall in our direction, nose in the air, smiling slightly to herself. She looked vaguely familiar, but I couldn't quite remember who she was. Then I heard one of the girls in the squad mutter, "Ricki Jennings! That girl thinks she's the greatest thing on earth."

I placed her then. Ricki was a sophomore, and she wasn't wildly popular with anyone. She'd attended some private girls academy near Harrisville before her family moved to Fieldcrest, and she never let anyone forget she thought she was lowering herself by associating with kids from our school. In just five days she'd won a name for herself as a grade-A snob, and even the seniors knew her by sight.

I turned away, forgetting about her until I heard a high-pitched voice trilling, "You're Mandy Birch, aren't you?"

When I turned around, Ricki was practically on top of me, smiling so cordially I wondered if maybe the kids hadn't been fair to her. She didn't seem so awful to me.

"That's right," I said. I smiled warmly, trying to make up for the kids who'd been rude to her since she started school here.

"Oh, you must think I'm so nervy!" she blurted

out. "I mean, barging in to say hello to someone I don't even know—and a cheerleader at that!"

I was about to say that I didn't think she had a nerve and it was perfectly all right. But Ricki didn't give me a chance to open my mouth before she plowed ahead enthusiastically. "It's just that I've heard so much about you," she explained. "Why, my cousin couldn't stop talking about what a hit you were at cheerleading camp."

All the other kids were silent now, listening. "Your cousin?" I echoed.

"My cousin, Joy," she said, and immediately I recognized the evil gleam in her eyes. "She said you and Mick Farris were the talk of the whole camp. Imagine!"—she turned to include the rest of the squad in her remark—"A Falcon falling in love with a Rattler! Love does conquer all, doesn't it?"

Then she was gone, leaving me too stunned to rush after her and pull her carefully combed black hair out by the roots. The silence around me was shattered by the bell's ringing, but nothing broke the stares aimed in my direction.

I swallowed hard. "Hey, I can explain—"

"Come on, everyone. We're late as it is." No one seemed to be looking at me as Keith moved forward and opened the door. Everyone just shuffled into the gym as if I weren't there. I followed

65

meekly, all my excitement about practice gone. Now what was I going to do?

Ms. Fairburn was our faculty adviser. Only a few years out of college—where she'd been a cheerleader—she was one of the girls' PE teachers. I'd had her for gym class the previous year, so I understood why the squad was so fond of her. She had more enthusiasm than ten Falcons' fans put together. She was already inside the gym, rolling out the thick practice mats. About half the squad rushed to help her; the other half murmured quietly among themselves as they took seats on the bottom bleachers. I stood frozen for a moment, not sure what to do. Did they expect me to sit off somewhere in a corner by myself?

Well, I'd be darned if I'd start acting like I was guilty of a crime! Taking a deep breath, I plopped myself down next to Bev as if that ugly scene with Ricki hadn't happened. She gave me a sidelong look. "Is it true, Mandy?" she whispered.

"Is the wonderful guy you met at camp really Mick Farris?"

"Yes," I admitted readily, glad to have the truth out at last, awkward as it may have been. "But it's not what you think. My loyalty is to Fieldcrest. Honest!"

"You should have told us, Mandy!" April hissed.

"Yeah, what's the big idea?" someone else chimed in. "Did you think we wouldn't discover you'd sold out?"

"I have *not* sold out!" I muttered, feeling my cheeks grow hot. "Going out with Mick has nothing to do with the squad!"

Whispering furiously, we must have sounded like a bank of leaking steam radiators. Ms Fairburn looked up, alert and curious as the rest of the squad joined us on the bleachers.

"What's going on?" she asked, her eyebrows raised. "Come on, gang, you've been whispering since you walked in here. Why doesn't someone let me in on it?"

At that, of course, we all suddenly got very preoccupied, looking at our feet, picking imaginary lint off our uniforms, doing anything to avoid answering the question.

Taking a deep breath, I got to my feet. Now, I decided, was the time to do what I should have done in the first place, to tell all.

"It's me, Ms. Fairburn," I announced, my voice strong if a little shaky. "While I was at cheerleading camp, I met Mick Farris, the co-captain of Roosevelt's cheering squad, and I started going out with him. I know I should have let everybody know, but I was afraid of what the reaction would be. Now somebody else just told everyone, and judging from the way everyone's acting, you can see I was right."

No one spoke as Ms. Fairburn paced back and forth, lost in thought. I sank back onto the bleacher, avoiding looking at anyone but her. For those brief moments, I saw my fate resting in her hands.

Finally she stopped and looked up, her glance sweeping over all of us. "Let's get this out in the open," she said evenly. "Do the rest of you feel that Mandy's compromised the squad in some way?"

I guess no one wanted to be the first to point an accusing finger at me. I was glad it was Keith's voice I heard first. He was known for his fairness and his cool head. If anyone was going to give me the benefit of the doubt, it would be Keith.

"I don't think any of us feels we have the right to tell somebody else who they should or shouldn't date," he said slowly. "But you've got to admit it's awfully sneaky to try to keep something like this hushed up. If Mandy isn't doing something wrong, why didn't she tell us she was dating Farris?"

"Mandy?"

"I don't know, Ms. Fairburn." I sighed deeply, then swiveled to face the squad. "I wanted to, honest I did. And I promised myself I'd never let

Mick interfere with my loyalty to Fieldcrest or my cheering. I was just so scared nobody would understand! He's a terrific person," I added, thinking it wouldn't hurt to put in a word or two in Mick's defense. "We've talked the whole thing over, and we both feel the same way—that being rivals doesn't mean we have to be hateful enemies."

"Maybe you're right." It was April's lilting voice agreeing reluctantly, and my spirits rose. "I'd hate for us to be accused of being poor sports and not showing the proper spirit toward a competitor. But Roosevelt! If only Mick went to some other school in the conference. Gosh, Mandy, you know how the kids feel about the Rattlers."

"How can we be sure you're not telling your boyfriend our secrets and our new cheers?" Will's deep bass challenged me. "How can we trust you when we know you'll be seeing him all the time?"

"Look," I said seriously, no longer avoiding their gazes but seeking them out in turn, "when I made the squad, I took the same pledge everyone of you took. I vowed to do my best for Fieldcrest and to put school spirit first. I take that vow seriously, and no one—not a boyfriend or anyone else—is going to make me break it. I don't see any reason why I don't deserve your trust. But"—I stopped, then steeled myself to speak the difficult words—"if the rest of you guys think I'm a traitor and don't want me on the squad, I'm not going to force you to let me stay."

Every cell in my body seemed to be quivering after I finished speaking. If they voted me off the squad, I'd be more miserable than I'd ever been in my entire life. Yet I knew I couldn't cheer with a bunch of kids who thought of me as a back stabber. If they really distrusted me that much, it was better to have it over with.

At first no one said a word, and I wondered if Ms. Fairburn was going to have to push them to make a decision. Then April spoke. "Look, we all know what a great job Mandy did for the J.V. squad last year. I certainly don't feel she'd ever do anything to hurt the Falcons. I hope everyone agrees."

To my great relief, the murmurs that followed April's remarks were in my favor.

"You can't quit the squad, Mandy!" Bev insisted, squeezing my arm so hard it hurt.

"We were shocked to hear about Mick Farris," a senior named Marsh added, "but that doesn't mean we want you off the squad."

Even Will joined in, looking sheepish since he was the one who'd come out with the closest thing to an outright accusation of disloyalty. "Yeah, we're not monsters, you know. Besides," he kidded, "we'd be fools for letting that camp scholarship go to waste, wouldn't we?"

People started laughing then, and the atmosphere lightened. It was Keith's remark that really clinched it. "Yeah, Mandy," he said, "just because you've got weird taste in men—" That was as far as he got. Everybody started whistling and shouting, "You said it!" At that moment I felt things were going to work out.

"OK, gang, have we got that settled now?" Ms. Fairburn, hands on hips, waited for everybody to agree that even though they thought I was nuts for dating someone from Roosevelt, they didn't actually believe I'd betray them. Then, with a nod of satisfaction, she said, "All right then, Mandy, why don't you come out here and show us all what you learned during that week at cheerleading camp. Besides how to disarm the enemy, that is."

The chuckles of my fellow squad members followed me as I walked out on the floor, giddy with relief. The crisis had come and gone. I could hardly wait to get home and phone Mick to tell him that the Falcon cheerleaders had given our romance, if not their blessing, at least their grudging approval.

Chapter Eight

Have you ever noticed that the more you want something to be all right, the harder you work at ignoring the signs that it isn't? That's how it was with me.

See, I kept telling myself that as long as the other cheerleaders weren't in favor of booting me off the squad, my relationship with Mick was an accepted thing that was never going to cause me to lose a moment's sleep. Ha!

Nothing went drastically wrong at first—that is, nothing happened that was bad enough to force me to admit all wasn't well.

For example, when the word spread around school that I was going out with the Rattlers' cheerleading co-captain, no one came right out and implied I wasn't to be trusted. As a matter of fact, lots of Fieldcrest students treated the news of my dating Mick like the happy, but not especially scandalous, news it was. It was the *others'* reactions that should have wised me up that it was going to be rough.

It was Moose Snyder, I think, who first started making remarks about Mick whenever we passed each other in the halls. And since Moose was star fullback on the football team, it wasn't long before the rest of the players were following his example and razzing the daylights out of me.

"Hey, what's the trouble, Mandy?" he asked one day, winking to show he was just kidding in spite of the harsh tone of his voice. "I hear you think the Falcons are too strong, so you had to go all the way to Roosevelt to find someone wimpy enough for you."

Get the picture?

Another time, while some of his buddies looked on and broke up, Moose begged, "You've got to help us, Mandy. We hear the Rattlers have worked up a dynamite new cheer. Can you use your influence to get us the lowdown?"

It was hardly funny, and if the joking had been about something else, I might have snapped back at him. But I was too scared of offending anyone to open my mouth. My fellow cheerleaders had given me their vote of confidence, so I wasn't about to do anything that might make them think I was disloyal.

Mick and I started to have troubles, too. The tension between us started building at our first game against Roosevelt, an away game in New Haven. Until then, everything was fine. The week before, both our schools had played our first football games on Saturday afternoon. Both our teams had won hands down, so Mick and I were in the best of moods. When we went out that night, just to make sure nothing went wrong, I suggested taking in a movie we'd both wanted to see. The fact that it was playing in neither New Haven nor Fieldcrest didn't hurt.

When Mick kissed me good night in front of my house, my heart threatened to burst through my ribs. "I can't believe you were here all this time and I'd never discovered you," he whispered, his lips brushing my hair. "Think of how much time we wasted!"

"We're not wasting it now," I assured him breathlessly.

Then, in a hushed tone that sent a shiver up my spine, Mick whispered, "I really think I love you, Mandy."

I *knew* I loved him. But before I could say the words, his lips were on mine again, and any desire I'd had to talk was forgotten.

The Roosevelt mixer was the following Friday, the night before our big game against each other, and I was nervous as I waited for Mick to pick me up. Though I'd been showered and dressed for ages, I couldn't sit down and relax.

I'd joined the family around the dinner table long enough to bolt down half a stuffed pork chop and some mashed potatoes. Then, since Mom had excused me from clean-up duties, I hurried back upstairs to touch up my makeup for the third time.

In my room I stopped pacing long enough to cast a critical eye at my reflection in the full-length mirror hanging on my closet door. What would Mick's friends from Roosevelt see? I wondered. Would they judge me on my own merits, or would they see me only as a Falcon, the enemy? It was impossible to relax with *that* hanging over me.

Mick didn't exactly appear calm as he picked me up, and he was unusually quiet on the drive to New Haven.

"Are you worried about how your friends will act toward me?" I finally asked.

"Of course not," he insisted, but he didn't sound very sure. "I just—oh, you know how keyed up everyone gets the night before a big game."

I murmured a vague answer, then turned up the volume on the radio. I didn't need any explanations about being keyed up. After all, I'd cheered at the Fieldcrest pep rally during school that day and seen the students shout even louder than usual. Some of the guys had stomped their feet on the bleachers so hard the wood threatened to give way, and Mr. Barrett, the football coach, had to ask everyone to take it easy. "Save some of that spirit for the game tomorrow!" he'd said, trying to make light of it. But the current running through the crowd wasn't mere school spirit, and Mr. Barrett knew it. The Falcons were out for the Rattlers' blood.

Considering that Roosevelt and Fieldcrest were mortal enemies, the reception I got at the mixer wasn't nearly so cool as it might have been. Oh, I wasn't blind to the little circles of students who stood around whispering between dances when Mick and I walked by. But most of Mick's friends had manners enough not to mention which school I attended and to keep the conversation off the subject of football, even if they did look a little uncomfortable at times. But I suppose Mick would have received the same sort of reception at Fieldcrest, and I knew it was a tribute to his own popularity that people bothered to talk to me at all.

It may sound as if I didn't have such a hot time, but that wasn't the case. I took the reaction of most of the Roosevelt kids as a good sign, or at least an optimistic one. The kids weren't openly hostile, so I was content with the hope that once they got used to seeing the two of us together, everything would be fine.

I was weak with nervousness when Mick introduced me to Troy Simon, his best friend. I was desperately afraid Troy wouldn't like me—and I knew it was important that he did. The fact that Troy was over six feet tall, with crisp black hair, intense dark eyes, and an air of sophistication made me feel even more anxious. I mean, anyone would have known that Troy was *somebody* by the way he stood out in that crowd of kids. He seemed so sure of himself and so worldly in his gray flannel slacks and tweed jacket that on him looked more casual than the sweaters and jeans most of the other guys wore.

It turned out that there was no reason to worry. In spite of his looks, Troy wasn't the least bit conceited, and the impishness of his generous smile when we were introduced made me sure I was going to get along with him. He even made a joke out of the famous rivalry, instead of awkwardly avoiding the subject.

I was puzzled at first when he reached out and rubbed the top of my head. Then I understood when he said, "Say, I don't feel any horns growing there! Guess not all the Fieldcrest gang are devils."

Laughter born of sheer relief bubbled out of my mouth, and even the Roosevelt kids nearby, who'd overheard Troy's remark, snickered. "I'm really normal," I assured Troy when I stopped laughing.

"You look more than normal to me, Mandy," he said, giving me an admiring once-over. "You look really good. But then, Mick and I have been friends since we were both in our cribs, so I wouldn't expect anything but good taste from him. If you've got any friends as cute as you, keep me in mind for a blind date."

Later, as Mick and I were driving home after leaving the dance early so we could both get a good night's sleep, I remarked on Troy's outgoing attitude.

"Oh, Troy's always thought this foes-to-the-death thing between Roosevelt and Fieldcrest was stupid," Mick said. "He's a stickler for what he believes in, sometimes to the point of pushing it too far. I mean, he'd love to go out with a girl fron Fieldcrest just to flaunt his independence in front of the other kids. He's always been a rebel."

"Is he on the football team?" I asked hopefully.

"No way! Troy's athletic and great in intramural sports, but he won't go out for any teams. Says he thinks the sports system should be abolished in high school because it takes away from academic subjects. Like I said, he was born a rebel."

"But the kids still like him, don't they?"

"Oh, sure, but no one takes Troy's opinions all that seriously. They've known him so long they expect him to say something's white if everyone else says it's black."

I'd have been a lot happier if my biggest supporter at Roosevelt was someone whose opinion carried more weight. But I'd liked Troy, and it was nice knowing somebody was on my side one hundred percent. If only everyone at Roosevelt and Fieldcrest could see things as Troy did!

The next day was bright, crisp, and cool, the kind of day people called "perfect football weather." Fall was in the air at last.

I met Bev at her house. She was my partner for a new cheer we'd be doing that day, and we wanted to practice our jumps a few more times before the game. In partner cheers it's important that the paired cheerleaders leave the ground and land at the same instant, and Bev and I had been having a little trouble with that. Now we worked at getting the routine down pat, then walked over to the school, where the buses bound for New Haven would soon be boarding in the parking lot.

The first game against Roosevelt was always a big deal, and this season was no exception. Seven school booster buses were lined up next to one another in the parking lot, three more than usual for an away game. Throngs of supporters, many wearing their gold and tan Falcon jackets, were already standing around waiting for the team to come out of the gym and board the team bus.

It wasn't hard to figure out that the team bus was the first one. Its yellow sides were covered with gold and tan bunting and signs proclaiming "Falcons #1," "Roust the Rattlers," "Fieldcrest Forever," and "Stomp the Snakes."

Bev and I joined the other cheerleaders, who were lining up in two columns facing one another by the first bus, forming a loose human hallway for the team to go through as they headed for the bus.

When the doors from the gym opened and the players started jogging in our direction, helmets dangling from their hands, the din was deafening. Any mixed emotions I'd had about Fieldcrest competing with Roosevelt evaporated as I warmed to the excitement. My voice was as loud as the others as I cheered on each individual player by name. And all the way to New Haven, I was enthusiastic in leading the fight songs. First and last, I was a Falcon, and I knew nothing could match the excitement of cheering at my first big varsity game against our most threatening opponents.

It was strange in a way, because I totally forgot about Mick until he took the field with the rest of the home team's cheering squad to lead the traditional welcoming cheer to the visiting team. I was much too preoccupied, trying to remember the order of our own cheers to think about him. I hadn't even sneaked a peek in the direction of the Roosevelt stands during the singing of our national anthem. My heart was firmly where it belonged—with my own team.

"Some welcome!" Will Hendricks, who was standing next to me at the foot of our bleachers snorted halfway through Roosevelt's cheer. "They couldn't sound more halfhearted if they were welcoming the plague."

When our turn came to reciprocate, April led us out onto the field. "Let's show those turkeys that our team spirit's more than skin deep!" she yelled. "Make it sound like we're really glad we're here!"

I was proud of Fieldcrest then. The Roosevelt stands may have been fuller than ours since it was their home game but our greeting cheer to them was double the volume theirs had been. I couldn't help but think we were all a little hypocritical, though. After all, we were shouting our lungs out about how glad we were to be there when the truth was we were glad only for the chance to slaughter them on the playing field. I guess Troy had a point when he insisted school competitions were stupid.

The game was an exciting one—at least what I saw of it was. To be honest, once the game started I was busier watching the other cheering squad than the battling football players. After all, the rival cheerleaders and not the players were *our* opponents.

I was impressed when their squad did a perfectly choreographed dance routine with one of their fight songs. It seemed awfully professional to me—or, I should say, that's how it seemed until Keith Watkins perched next to me on the edge of the bottom bleacher where I'd sat to rest for a minute.

"They look like a bunch of fools, don't they?" he remarked. "Don't they know the difference between a football game and a Broadway musical?"

"You're not kidding!" I agreed enthusiastically, forgetting that a moment earlier I'd been thinking how good they looked. "We're here to cheer, not do a lot of high kicks like the Rockettes."

"Your boyfriend's not bad, though. Too bad he always shifts his legs to the left like that on his back jumps. Makes him look a little lopsided."

Needless to say, I watched Mick as critically as I watched the rest of his squad. I was proud of his talent on the field, but I didn't want him to look a lot better than I did. And I couldn't help but feel a little pang of jealousy when I noticed he was paired off with the same leggy redhead during all the partner cheers. It didn't seem fair that he got to partner with a pretty girl while I cheered with Bev. And I wasn't any happier when I took a good look at the way she hugged him after one of the routines. Maybe he was a Rattler, but he was still *my* boyfriend.

The score was close all afternoon. It wasn't until the fourth quarter that Fieldcrest got the touchdown that would win the game. After that, I didn't bother watching Mick anymore. All I cared about was doing my best to keep our team's spirits from flagging so Roosevelt wouldn't sneak in and tie the score. As we counted down the last ten seconds on the time clock, our voices were high with triumph. The Fieldcrest boosters were frantic with excitement. In a matter of seconds, everyone from the bleachers seemed to be down on the field, hugging and dancing around the players, who were tossing their helmets high in the air.

It wasn't until I was clapping to one of our victory songs on the bus that I wondered if I should have made an effort to find Mick before we left. But, no, I thought. It would have been impossible with so many people surging around. Besides, I'd be seeing him at eight-thirty when he picked me up at home. By then, I was certain he'd be over any disappointment he might be feeling about Roosevelt's losing. It never even occurred to me that this date might not be like any of the others.

Chapter Nine

I'd just removed the electric rollers from my hair when I heard the doorbell ring. Rushing to the top of the stairs, I called down, "Mom, if that's Mick, tell him I'll be right there, would you please?"

My freshly washed and ironed jeans and tan turtleneck jersey were draped across my bed, where I'd set them out earlier. I wriggled into them, slipped on my loafers, then pulled a brush through my hair. After giving my lipstick a final touch-up and quick blot, I pulled on my tweed blazer, flung my shoulder bag over my arm, and dashed down the stairs.

Mick was seated at the dining room table with Mom and Dad, a piece of my mother's superdelicious french apple pie half eaten on the plate in front of him and a glass of milk in his hand. Mom and Dad were having coffee, though I noticed Dad's eyes staring hungrily at the half of the pie that remained in the pie tin.

"Go on, Dad," I said, slouching into the chair across from Mick. "You look like a cat watching a mouse, so why don't you have some?"

"If I were your age, I would," he said seriously. "But I'm a man pushing into middle age, and the spare tire I've gathered along the way has got to go. Much as I love your mother's pies, one slice after dinner's got to do for me."

"It sure is delicious, Mrs. Birch." Mick pushed away his plate, empty now, then swallowed the last of his milk. "I wish my mom could bake like that."

"She's not a baker?"

"Says she doesn't have the knack." He grinned. "Her pie crusts usually taste like cardboard, so I guess she's telling the truth. But she does make a mean rice pudding."

"Don't tell me the three of you have been sitting here talking about all sorts of wonderfully fattening things while I was upstairs squeezing myself into my jeans!" I teased.

"Actually we were talking about football," Dad explained, taking a paper napkin and unfolding it across the pie tin so he wouldn't be tempted any longer.

"Football?" I'd been hoping to avoid the subject, but since it was being thrust on me, I felt I had to make a comment. "The Rattlers sure played a great game today. It was touch and go all the way."

"We were talking about the *pro* game that's on TV tomorrow," Mick said, giving me what almost amounted to a dirty look. "You know, Mandy, not everyone's as obsessed by Roosevelt-versus-Fieldcrest as the Falcons are."

"Oh." I didn't know what else to say, hurt that Mick had spoken to me in such a harsh tone when I was just trying to be polite. I don't know how long the four of us would have sat there in silence if Mom hadn't suddenly asked Mick brightly, "Did Mandy tell you Real's band has a job tonight? A 'gig,' as Jo calls it?"

"No, but that's great. Where's he playing?" He asked the question in my general direction.

"Pete's Pizza out on the New Haven road," I said. "I guess *they* won't be doing a red-hot business tonight."

"The band doesn't sound that bad to me," Dad put in unexpectedly. "Not so bad as some of those groups on MTV. And I certainly prefer their music to their name."

"How come?" I asked. "I don't think Real could have come up with a more fitting name for the group than Capital Punishment. The only name that might be more appropriate would be A Fate Worse Than Death."

"Give the poor kid a chance, Mandy!" Mick was laughing now, and I wondered if maybe I'd just imagined that almost dirty look. "After all, he's an artist. He's expressing himself."

"If that's self-expression, then some things are better left unexpressed," I retorted.

"And some things," Mom said, pulling the pie tin out of the way just before Dad's hand reached it, "are better left uneaten."

"Guess I'm going to have to be good in spite of myself." Dad pushed himself away from the table. "I don't know if whatever's on TV is going to be good enough to keep my mind off your apple pie, Maureen, but I'll have to give it a shot."

We all stood up then, Mick thanking Mom for the snack while I went into the kitchen with his dirty dishes and the rest of the pie.

"Have a good time," Mom said as we headed for the front door.

"And if you end up at the pizza parlor," Dad added with a wink, "have a slice with pepperoni on it for me."

"Did your sister go to hear the band?" Mick asked as he started the car.

"Are you kidding? This is her moment of glory. She'll be glued to a ringside seat."

"Want to head over that way?"

"To hear Real?" I swiveled to face Mick in surprise. "When I've got to listen to his idea of music all the time in my own house? Thanks, but no thanks."

"What'll it be then?" Mick asked, slowly guiding the car away from the curb. "The Burger Barn? Or do you want to go out to the arcade at the mall? I heard they got some new video games in the last week."

"Before you came over, April Adams called," I told him. "She's the captain of our squad, and she said she was having some kids over. Nothing special. Just Cokes and records. But we're invited if we want to go."

"Thanks, but no thanks." Mick mimicked what I'd said before, sounding every bit as sarcastic as I had.

"Why not?" I was confused. "How are you ever going to get on good terms with my friends if you don't even meet them?"

"Look, Mandy, I'm more than willing to get to know every last soul at Fieldcrest, and I'm sure I'll like more of them than I won't, but I'm not exactly thrilled at the prospect of sitting around while a bunch of Falcon cheerleaders celebrate their victory over my school's team. So, if you don't mind, let's not."

Well, I did mind. April was a senior and head of the cheering squad, and I was glad when she called me at home and invited me over. But instead of blurting out how I felt, I tried to put myself in Mick's shoes and realized that I couldn't blame him.

"Let's go to the arcade then," I suggested. "If the Rattlers had creamed us on the field today, I don't suppose I'd be eager to go to a Roosevelt party myself."

It was dark, too dark for me to see Mick's features, but when he spoke his words had the sound of being forced through clenched teeth. "The Rattlers weren't exactly creamed. It was a single touchdown difference as I recall."

"I didn't mean it that way. Honest," I assured him. Then I leaned back against the worn seat cushions and sighed. If Mick was going to be oversensitive, that was his problem. I just hoped he snapped out of it before the night was a total washout.

He seemed OK when we parked at the mall and headed for the arcade. I took his hand, lacing my fingers through his, and he bent down to nuzzle the top of my head with his lips. I should have known Mick wasn't the type to let a bad mood grab hold of him.

Even though Mick was crazy about the war games and space machines, he gave in to me so we could play my favorite first. I liked the jungle game best. You know the one I mean, I'm sure. First, you have to make a little guy swing from vine to vine, then swim through the water and knife the alligators, then race up the hill without getting hit by the boulders rolling down before he gets his chance to rescue the damsel in distress from cannibals.

As usual, Mick was in top form. He got all the way to the boulder part before his first slipup. Then it was my turn. I don't know what it was, just being worn out from all the excitement of the afternoon and the night before, I guess, but I just couldn't get it together. I missed on the third vine jump, overshooting the mark, and my little man fell down on the ground with that awful computerized clunk.

"Well, some days you have it, and some days you don't," I murmured, turning the controls back to Mick.

"Maybe spending all day with the Falcon cheering squad made some of their lack of coordination rub off on you," Mick said, his eyes on the screen, where he nimbly dodged boulders.

"What's that supposed to mean? At least nobody on my squad sticks their legs way out to the left when they do a back jump. We may not have the greatest coordination, but we aren't lopsided."

I heard Mick's deep breath as a boulder flattened the little man on the game screen. "Very funny," he said dryly. "If you're so great at jumping, this time why don't you try jumping the vines without crashing onto the ground?"

"Listen, I don't want to have a fight over your lame cheering squad," I told him, jumping from vine to vine with the kind of concentration usually reserved for brain surgery, then sighing with relief when the vines faded out and the water appeared on the screen. "I don't mean that *you're* lame. But how did you get stuck doing so many partner stunts with that fat redhead? Or did they figure they needed a big guy with a lot of muscle to heave her off the ground?" I took my eyes off the screen to watch Mick's reaction and heard the fate of the little video man as a crocodile did him in.

"You sound jealous." Mick slipped past me and took his place at the controls again. "But I can see being jealous of Fran—who, by the way, hasn't got an ounce of fat on her body. Yeah, I can understand how another girl could envy Fran's gorgeous hair and her great figure. Of course, I could never be jealous of that goofy-looking guy who was watching you all afternoon."

"What guy was that, smarty?"

"The tall, skinny one. Boy, is he ever weird-looking!"

"Keith Watkins is not weird-looking!" I protested. "And he is not interested in me. He's going out with my best friend."

"Your girlfriends have strange taste in men."

I giggled. "That's funny. That's exactly what Keith said about me."

Scowling, Mick stopped playing and put his hands in his pockets, just watching as another boulder ended his turn. "This game's stupid," he said. "Come on, let's go get something to drink. Then we can play some of the *good* games."

"But we haven't finished playing!" I grabbed the controls for my last turn. "I don't want to waste money."

Out of the corner of my eye, I could see Mick shrugging. "Take my turn, too, if it means that much to you. I'll be at the snack bar when you're done."

He walked away without looking back.

Of course I lost my turn and his instantly. How could I be expected to concentrate when he'd done everything in his power to upset me? When I let go of the controls, my hands were sweaty and shaky. I couldn't believe Mick had talked to me that way! I gritted my teeth, fished in my purse for more quarters, and headed over to good old reliable Pac-Man. There was no way I'd go chasing after Mick.

I'd used up a dollar when it occurred to me

that Mick might not even bother coming to find me. So, swallowing my pride, I stomped off in the direction of the refreshment area. I was boiling, shocked, and angry that Mick—who'd made such a point of being above spiteful competition—was acting like such a baby just because Roosevelt had lost the game. On top of that, I was scared. Did he care so little about me that he'd just go off and leave me stranded at the arcade?

When I spotted Mick, my fear vanished, and my fury grew. Why, he appeared to have forgotten about me! He was standing at the counter, drinking something and talking animatedly to two guys who looked a few years older than us. It was all I could do not to burst into tears as I approached them, taking in every casual, relaxed gesture of Mick's every laugh and shrug. He wasn't acting at all like a boy who was worried about where his girlfriend had gone.

He looked over as I came up beside him. "Oh, here you are," he said easily, as if I'd been gone just a second or two. "Mandy Birch, this is Roger Hartley and Hal Gleason. They graduated from Roosevelt the same year your brother was sprung from Fieldcrest."

Roger, a big, brawny guy with an unexpectedly meek manner, said, "You're Terry Birch's sister? What's he up to these days?"

Trying to keep my voice from shaking, I explained he was stationed in Germany in the service.

"He was some athlete," Roger said sincerely. "Of course, I never got to know him all that well since he was the competition and all that, but I had a lot of respect for him as a team player."

"Yes," I said sweetly, "I know how seriously you Rattlers take competition."

He and Hal forced a chuckle, while Mick glared at me. "Just with Fieldcrest," Hal said, trying to turn the whole thing into a compliment. "The Falcons always did give Roosevelt a run for the money. Heard it was a really close game today."

"Not really," I corrected him, keeping my voice saccharine sweet. "I don't think there was ever any doubt who was going to win the game."

Neither of them seemed to know what to say to that. The four of us just stood there like statues until Roger finally cleared his throat and said, "Well, Mick, we'd better get going. Have to drive back to campus. Nice meeting you, Mandy."

His smile struck me as apologetic and regretful, filling me with shame even as it made me more angry at Mick. His former classmates thought I was a shrew, which was exactly what I'd acted like, and it was all Mick's fault. He was the one who'd shattered my perfectly good mood.

"It was nice meeting you, too," I said, my smile

more genuine this time. "You'll have to excuse me if I'm grouchy. It's been a long day."

"We all know what those are like!" Hal said easily, but as they wandered off, I couldn't help feeling they were glad to get away.

"Jeez, you sure know how to make a guy feel good in front of his friends!" Mick slammed his empty paper cup down on the counter. "Come on, let's get out of here."

Neither of us talked as we stomped across the parking lot to his car. *This is it,* I was thinking. The end of a perfect romance, which had turned out to be not so perfect after all. Well, it was better that I'd found out what a rotten sport Mick was before it was too late. To think I'd fallen for all that business about our "chemistry" being more important than rivalry. Too late I remembered it was simple chemistry that made bombs explode.

Without even asking whether or not I wanted to go home, Mick started driving in that direction. "I thought you wanted to go hear Real's band," I said innocently.

"You didn't want to go anyway, and I'm not in the mood anymore," he answered, his voice tight. "I think I'd rather head back to New Haven."

I sat stewing in silence for a minute, then said, "In that case, you may as well drop me on Laurel

Crescent instead of at my house. Take the first left after the traffic light up here."

"What's there?" he asked, his voice taut with challenge. But he made the left turn.

"Oh, it's April's house," I said offhandedly, keeping my voice bland. "As long as you're not feeling up to anything, I thought I may as well catch the last half of her party."

Mick didn't say another word as I continued giving him directions, but in the hazy light that filtered through the windshield from the overhead streetlights, I could see that his lips were compressed into a thin, tight line, while a little muscle twitched under his right cheekbone. When I pointed out April's brightly lit house, he cut over to the curb and put the brakes on sharply. "Here you are," he said. "Have a swell time."

"Thank you," I replied coldly. "I'm sure I will." Without as much as a glance at him, I jumped out of the car and slammed the door hard. As I stormed up the walk to the front door, Mick gunned the motor and took off down the street.

I was glad he'd zipped off because I needed a few seconds to compose myself before I rang the bell; I wouldn't have wanted him to see that I wasn't rushing to the door.

In the glow of the porch light, I slipped my makeup case out of my purse and patted powder across my nose, which was bright with the effort of holding back my tears. I added a quick slash of lipstick, then rang the bell. I knew there was about one chance in a million of my actually having anything approaching a good time, but I swore that no one would know I wasn't.

April answered the door herself. "Mandy! Great!" she welcomed me. "Come in, the party's just getting off the ground." She looked behind me as I passed through the doorway. "Where's Mick?"

"Poor thing! He was so tired he wanted to turn in early for a change. All this driving back and forth to be with me, you know." I sounded so sincere I was startled. Dishonesty had never been my big talent, but under the circumstances, I'd rather have told a thousand lies than look like a fool.

"That's too bad," April said sympathetically. "Follow me. The kids are all in the family room at the back of the house."

"Yes, as a matter of fact, Mick asked me to thank you for inviting him and apologize for not making it." I felt a warped satisfaction as I imagined the expression on Mick's face if he could hear me right then. "He was really looking forward to meeting all of our cheerleaders, you know. Said he was awfully impressed with what he saw this afternoon. He thinks a lot of our squad."

"Really?" April stopped to turn toward me, looking impressed. "He said all that about his biggest rivals? Wow! He must be something else!"

"Oh, he is," I agreed warmly. "He really is." To myself I added, *And whatever that something else is, I don't want to have any more to do with it.*

Chapter Ten

It wasn't long after midnight when Will Hendricks dropped me off, but the house was dark except for the hall light. Mom and Dad had turned in early, and grown-up though she thought she was, Jo's curfew was eleven o'clock on weekends; so I knew she, too, was snug in her bed. That was fine with me. I was in a terrible mood when I got home, and I was glad not to have to explain it to anyone.

I didn't think I'd sleep a wink that night, but I guess the events of the past two days had taken their toll. I was bone weary, and I could barely keep my eyes open while I scrubbed off my makeup and brushed my teeth. I must have dozed off the instant my head hit the pillow.

When I finally opened my eyes the next morning, the clock radio on the table next to my bed said ten o'clock, and I had that groggy, dazed feeling that comes from too much sleep.

I lay back against the pillow, waiting for my head to clear. Beneath the layers of sleep floated the feeling that something was wrong, but it took me a minute or two to remember what it was. Even then it hit me only because I was lazily thinking I should call Mick.

Mick! I sat bolt upright, suddenly wide awake and miserable. How could I have forgotten that awful scene of the night before? Of course I wouldn't be calling Mick. I'd never be calling him again.

Tears threatened to well up in my eyes, and if I'd stayed in bed, I knew I would have gotten very weepy. Instead, I gathered up all my willpower and headed downstairs. My self-respect, I knew, was more important than any boy.

"Well, sleepyhead, you must have painted the town last night," Mom greeted me as I entered the kitchen.

"Mmmmm," I answered noncommittally. "Oooh, would you mind making some more of those for me?" I asked as she expertly flipped two buttermilk pancakes onto the plate in front of Jo at the breakfast nook. "I'm ravenous!"

Through the window over the sink, I could see Dad hard at work cutting back and covering the rose bushes. *It's just a typical Sunday*, I reminded myself. *It's not the end of the world.*

I poured a small glass of orange juice and a

101

bigger tumbler of milk, then sat down. For once, I was thrilled to see Jo sprawled at the table—anything to keep my mind off Mick.

"How was rock 'n' roll heaven?" I asked her.

Jo tore her attention away from the pancakes she was devouring long enough to make a face at me. "As a matter of fact, it was great," she said coolly. "Some guy who books bands all over the East Coast was there, and he told Real he was very impressed. If Capital Punishment's still together by the summer, he thinks he can get them bookings on the road."

"That's nice," I murmured, flipping through the Sunday paper till I found the comics. Normally I'd have made some smart remark, like asking if the guy knew that Real would have to get permission from his mother to leave the town limits, but that day my heart wasn't in it. Even "Peanuts" didn't hit my funny bone the way it usually did.

Mom handed me a plate of pancakes, and I wasted a few minutes slathering them with butter and syrup. "These are even better than your apple pie," I told her as I dug in.

I almost choked on the mouthful I was swallowing when she said mildly, "Do you think so? I wonder if Mick would agree."

I shoveled more food into my mouth so I

wouldn't have to talk. Then she did it again. "Oh, speaking of Mick—"

This time I actually had a coughing spasm. When it died down, I took a big swallow of milk to clear my windpipe and asked, "Speaking of Mick, what?"

"Both you girls shouldn't take such big mouthfuls when you eat."

"What about Mick?" I prodded her, the suspense unbearable.

"Oh, he called earlier. I told him you were sleeping, and he said you should call him when you got up."

"Mick called?" I mumbled, not believing my ears.

"That's not surprising, is it, dear?" Mom gave me a curious look. "Maybe you'd better take a shower and wake up."

"Is that all he said? To call him?"

"No. He mentioned again how much he'd enjoyed the apple pie."

By then I was barely listening. I was too busy wolfing down the rest of my pancakes so I could closet myself in the den and return Mick's call.

But when I actually had the receiver in my hand, I wasn't in such a big hurry anymore. What would I say when Mick answered? I wondered. And why was he calling anyway? What if he'd called just to have the chance to say something mean about April's party? I dialed his number, then quickly hung up before his phone even had a chance to ring. I took a moment to pull myself together, then I dialed again.

The phone rang once, twice, three times, my stomach contracting in tempo with each ringing signal. What if Mick wasn't home anymore? I doubted I could get up the nerve to call again.

On the fourth ring Mick himself picked up.

"Hi—it's Mandy," I said slowly in response to his hello. "My mom said you called before."

"Yeah." There was an awful pause—it couldn't have been more than a few seconds, but it seemed like an eternity—then he said, "Look, Mandy, I wanted to say I'm sorry about last night. I had no right to snap your head off like that."

"Well, I guess it was my fault, too," I admitted, my anger replaced by a wave of gratitude toward Mick for being the first to say he was sorry. "I wasn't exactly a bundle of joy myself."

"Weird, wasn't it? I thought about it when I got home, and I realized it could have been a couple of strangers talking and not us. Didn't we promise we'd never let our schools come between us? I can't believe I didn't admit to myself how bothered I was at losing to Fieldcrest."

"Yeah," I agreed. "All that time we were worried about how the other kids would act, and

104

then it turned out to be you and me who were poor sports. I had a lousy time at April's party, too. And the worst part was, everyone was really disappointed you didn't make it. I lied and said you wished you could have gone."

I was afraid Mick would be mad, but he just chuckled softly. "That's just as well. I'd rather everyone else didn't know how stupid we were."

"I guess we're going to have to make more of an effort not to compete," I suggested. "I'd hate to think we were willing to break up over who could jump the highest."

"Or whose back jump was lopsided," Mick put in, but I could tell by the tone of his voice he wasn't mad at me anymore for my catty remark. We talked for a half hour more, then hung up, both glad that we hadn't let the previous night ruin our relationship.

It sounds like a happy ending, doesn't it? I just wish it had all been that simple. But it wasn't, not at all.

The following weekend Roosevelt played an away game Friday night, and we played another school at home on Saturday, so that meant we could go to both games and wouldn't have to worry about competing against each other. But it didn't matter because we'd promised never to be so childish again, not even when our schools competed.

That Friday night Mick picked me up early. We went to meet Troy for burgers and Cokes at a place not far from Roosevelt. Mick left to hook up with the rest of the Rattler squad, while Troy and I took our time finishing our sodas, then walked over to the game together.

"It feels funny to be sitting in the Roosevelt cheering section," I confessed as the players came onto the field.

"It shouldn't," Troy said pointedly. "The whole Falcon-Rattler thing's been way out of hand ever since I can remember. And the adults are as bad as the kids, egging everyone on to detest the other side. That'd never work in pro sports, you know. What would a guy do when he was traded off to the team he'd spent years hating?"

"You're right," I answered, but my mind wasn't on the conversation anymore. It was on the Roosevelt cheering squad down below us. After the last weekend I'd been sure that Mick, as co-captain, would be careful not to partner himself off with Fran anymore, knowing I hadn't liked it. Therefore, I was rattled to see him and the limber redhead, a solid twosome for every paired cheer.

"Mick and that girl make a good couple," I said brightly, wishing it weren't the truth. At least I'd managed to keep the jealousy I felt out of my voice.

"Oh, you mean Fran?" Troy asked absent-mindedly, his attention focused on the scrimmage that ended in a first down for the Rattlers. "There's nothing she'd like better than to *be* a couple," he remarked offhandedly. "I guess she's had a crush on Mick ever since grade school. Their folks used to spend summers at the same spot on the New Jersey shore when they were kids."

"That's right. Mick did say something about that," I said, wondering why Mick had never said anything about that.

Troy must have heard the doubt in my voice because he turned and gave my shoulder a playful pat. "Don't worry, kid. He's not the least bit interested in Fran."

I just smiled stiffly and turned my attention back to the field below us. I knew deep down that Troy was right; if Mick had had any interest in Fran, he never would have hooked up with me in the first place. But I still didn't like the fact that he was her partner in so many cheers, especially since I'd made it clear to him that I didn't approve.

Mick and I didn't exactly argue in his car on the way to the postgame party, but it wouldn't be stretching the point to say we bickered. As subtly as possible I brought up the subject of Fran, saying I'd expected him to be cheering with some of the other girls. "You've got to spread yourself around, you know," I said in an attempt at light-heartedness.

He shrugged, his hands staying on the steering wheel. "Fran and I look best together. We've tried different pairs but the way it is now is the way that works best."

"I just think you're a better cheerleader than she is," I said sweetly, hoping flattery might work.

Fat chance! "All the more reason I should give her a break," Mick answered smoothly.

"Look," I said less sweetly, my patience wearing thin, "If I were stuck cheering with someone everybody knew was hung up on me, would you like it?"

"Ah, so that's it! Old Troy told you, huh? So Fran has a crush on me, so what? I've kind of looked out for her ever since we were little kids, so why should I stop now? That's got nothing to do with you and me. Besides, I don't see how I could feel jealous if any of those Falcons were hung up on you. They're all such nerds I know you wouldn't give any of them the time of day."

"You know what I mean, Mick, so don't try to get out of giving me an explanation by acting like it's all a big joke!"

"What am I supposed to be explaining? I

already told you, Fran and I make a good couple. It's how we look on the field that's important, not how my girlfriend feels. Anyway, didn't we agree we weren't going to get uptight about anything to do with cheering?"

The exasperation I could hear beneath his calm tone snapped me to my senses. He was right, of course. Mick had his thing to do, and I had mine, and if it bothered me to watch him with Fran, maybe I shouldn't go to any more of Roosevelt's games.

"I'm not uptight, I promise." I snuggled closer to him. "I just wish it were me down there with you, I guess."

"Just remember, *you're* the one I meet after the game. Not Fran." He gave me a kiss as he braked for a stop sign, and that was that.

It was a good night. The Rattlers had won by a large margin, and all the Roosevelt kids were in high spirits. And since they hadn't been playing the Falcons, none of the kids seemed to think twice about my being from Fieldcrest. I was sure Mick and I finally had this school rivalry thing beat.

But the next day I wasn't so sure anymore. Mick came to watch Fieldcrest play Lincoln High, bringing Troy with him. Fieldcrest won easily, and afterward I took Mick and Troy to

April's house, the scene of the regular postgame get-together.

At first everything was fine. Mick was going out of his way to be friendly to all the kids I introduced him to, and I was willing to bet that easygoing Troy would have fit in anywhere in the world.

Things started getting tense when Keith came over and said to me, "You know, you were right about putting that new jump of yours in, Mandy. The crowd seemed crazy about that routine."

"Thanks, Keith. I'm glad April agreed to let me do it."

"You mean that straddle jump where you touched your toes?" Mick asked. "I liked it, too. Looked even better when you did it than when I came up with it to win the competition at camp."

"Don't make it sound like I stole your unique jump." I tried to banter, but the edge that undercut my words reached even my own ears. "I mean, that's a common jump, Mick. Lots of people do it all the time."

"Funny," he said innocently. "I never saw it before. And I thought I'd invented it." He winked at Keith. "Guess the joke's on me, huh?"

"Guess so," Keith agreed. "I never saw it before Mandy did it for us at practice, but I know she's too good a cheerleader to have to steal someone else's routine—especially a Rattler's."

Well, I could feel Mick stiffening next to me at that remark, and I couldn't tell if Keith had said it innocently or if he was trying to pick a fight. Knowing Keith, I was pretty sure it was without malice, but Mick's reaction could mean trouble. I grasped his forearm and started pulling him away. "Come on, let's get some refills on these sodas. Cheering in the sun all day's really made me thirsty."

It wasn't long afterward that Mick, who'd grown quiet, said he'd had enough of the party and suggested we go. "I'll hunt up Troy," he said, leaving me to make a circuit of the room saying goodbye to everyone.

As the three of us walked down the path to the car, I could tell by the straight set of Mick's shoulders that Keith's remark had upset him. "You don't really think I'd purposely steal something you'd created on your own, do you?" I asked him softly as I held the front seat forward for Troy to slip into the back. "I suppose maybe unconsciously I remembered part of your routine from the competition and worked it into the cheer. But you don't really think I'd come right out and steal from you, do you?"

"Of course not." He laughed bitterly. "Why

would a fabulous Falcon stoop so low as to steal something from a Rattler?"

Either Troy didn't pick up that something was wrong or he was busily trying to smooth things over. In either case, he didn't stop talking once during the ride to my house, which was just as well; Mick didn't give the slightest indication of wishing to share any of his thoughts, and I was afraid to voice mine. Why waste my breath telling him Keith hadn't meant anything malicious when Mick clearly preferred sulking? And why keep trying to convince him of what was true, that I probably had picked up bits of his cheering routine at camp but that I hadn't done it on purpose? I'd learned to hold my tongue about certain things.

When we arrived at my house, Mick walked me to the front door, where I kissed him good night as warmly as ever. I knew his whole fit of sullenness and sensitivity would blow over by the next day.

I was right about that, but in the weeks to come, it seemed as if neither Mick nor I missed a chance to pick at each other about cheering. And afterward I always wondered what had happened to our promise that we'd never let it come between us. Forget about Fieldcrest and Roosevelt being rivals—our own personal competition was enough to put a damper on our relationship.

Sometimes I thought it might even be better if we actually came right out and fought. But we never got that far. I know on my part, at least, I never brought up the rivalry on purpose. I'd just open my mouth, intending to say something innocent, and instead, some snide remark about Roosevelt's cheering squad would sneak out. And I knew Mick was trying just as hard not to be cutting or critical, but sometimes he, too, would slip. Sooner or later, of course, we'd both forget about whatever unimportant thing it was we'd been bickering about. But it was still a strain, and more than once I almost canceled a date, afraid of what Mick might say that evening.

I was confused and made weary by the whole thing. It seemed years since I'd felt one hundred percent relaxed with Mick, free to talk about whatever crossed my mind. Now, I had to think carefully before speaking.

The possibility of quitting the squad crossed my mind a few times, but I wouldn't even consider it, not seriously. Being a cheerleader was one of the best parts of my life. I just couldn't give it up, not for *any* boy.

But what could I do? The tension between us wasn't lessening, not a bit. Every week I felt it grow. I knew that sooner or later the situation had to reach a point where everything would just go snap! And it did, the very next time the Rattlers and the Falcons got together on the football field.

Chapter Eleven

Our second game against Roosevelt was played at Fieldcrest. That's the tradition in our football conference, that the teams take turns playing host to the opponent. It was a Saturday afternoon game in late October.

Maybe it was because Halloween was drawing near or maybe because deep down inside I knew that things between Mick and me would get worse; in any case, I was filled with a sense of foreboding for the entire week preceding the contest—a dreadful premonition that something would happen. I was so uneasy that I called off my date with Mick the night before the game, saying I had a slight sore throat and didn't want to take my chance on being hoarse the next day.

Saturday dawned overcast, and the only bright spot was the possibility that the skies might split open in a torrential rainstorm, making things so wet the game would be postponed.

"Looks like rain," I remarked, trying not to sound too hopeful as I sat around the dining room table with my folks at lunch. Jo was off someplace with her superstar-to-be. "I wouldn't be surprised if we had a storm."

"Not a chance." The certainty in Dad's voice sent my hopes crashing to the ground. "The barometer says not, anyhow. So does my ankle. It's felt fine all morning." Dad had broken his ankle before I was even born, and the twinges he felt in it when rain was on the way were always accurate.

"Well, it sure *looks* like rain," I said listlessly.

"And it sure looks as if one young lady isn't going to eat the second half of her sandwich," Dad hinted.

"You go ahead and take it," I told him. "I shouldn't eat much if I'm going to be jumping around later on."

"But, honey, you hardly touched the first half. You're not catching cold, are you?"

Mom went to lay the back of her hand against my forehead to check for a fever, but I leaned away from her, sliding out of my chair. "I feel fine," I assured her. "Just keyed up for the game, you know."

Then, before either of them could ask if something was bothering me, I hurried away explaining, "I'd better get started on cleaning up my room if I want to get it done before I've got to leave."

Upstairs, I put an old Police tape on, then attacked my bedroom. I would have cleaned the whole house from top to bottom to wipe away the horrible image that kept flashing in my mind—of Mick and me standing, hands on our hips, our faces contorted and twisted with hatred, screeching at each other across a totally empty football field.

Housework didn't seem like such drudgery to me whenever I did it to avoid thinking of something else. Now my tidying up had the intensity of an addiction. I dragged the vacuum cleaner from the hall closet and steered it across every square inch of carpeting, polished the furniture until it gleamed, put every stray book, record, and tape I owned back in alphabetical order. Then, seeing I still had a good hour and a half before Bev would be stopping by to pick me up, I started on my dresser drawers and my closet, sorting out jumbled socks and rolling them up into pairs, discarding panty hose with runs in them, refolding T-shirts and jeans, and hanging up everything that had fallen on the floor.

It was while I was going through my bottom dresser drawer that I discovered, way at the back under a pile of summer clothes, my bright red and white C.C.A. top and shorts.

I sat cross-legged on the floor, gazing at them. I let myself sink into a reverie, turning camp memories over and over in my mind like precious jewels. There I was, slouching into the grandstand area, reluctant to join the others who were still strangers, when I looked up and into Mick's eyes as he watched me with interest. I saw him getting to his feet in the cafeteria to introduce himself to the group, feeling first the shock of recognition as I realized he was from Roosevelt, then the pang of pleasure as he crossed the room in my direction. I melted into his arms in the spot hidden from the other campers at the parking lot rally.

I lifted the crumpled outfit against my cheek, as if it were a magic pillow on which I could dream away all the tension and strain that had seeped into my relationship with Mick. Then I closed my eyes tight and wished with all my might that nothing would ever happen to destroy all the wonderful times we still could have together. If we could just make it through the rest of the football season! The rivalry between our two schools wasn't nearly so poisonous in other team sports.

The click of my tape deck switching itself off snapped me out of my daze. I looked at the balled-up outfit clutched in my hand and shook my head, laughing without much humor. If anybody could see me making wishes on a cotton jersey, they'd probably send for a straitjacket!

Then, tossing my camp uniform back into the drawer, I crossed to the closet and took out the uniform I'd be wearing that day. I was still proud of my cheering outfit, still felt special and singled out from the crowd when I was wearing it. But as I put it on that day, my pleasure was mixed with reluctance. I'd have been more at peace if the game had been called off and the uniform left to hang in the closet for another week.

As we cheerleaders ran in single file to the front of the Fieldcrest bleachers, I could hear the buzz of the capacity crowd and feel the current of anticipation running through them. This game was important not only because it was our first meeting with Roosevelt on our home ground, but it also marked the halfway point in the football conference; whoever won would have an edge in qualifying for the division play-offs.

The first two quarters went well. The teams played neck and neck, which kept me much too busy to worry about what the other squad was doing. Caught up in the enthusiasm of the crowd and the closeness of the score, I forgot my earlier premonition and gave myself up to the exhilaration of cheering. For the time being, my love of leading cheers and my determination to whip up school spirit overshadowed everything else. At one point I even wondered how I could have dreaded going to the game.

We always had halftime shows, with each school's marching band and cheerleaders taking the field in turn. This day, because our game with Roosevelt was the most highly attended and most critical, we'd planned an extravaganza, which we'd rehearsed every day after school. Since we were scheduled to go on first at halftime, we took turns leaving the field one by one during the final minutes of the second quarter. It was our only chance to grab a quick drink of water or to dash into the rest room.

When my turn came, I grabbed my purse from where I'd stuck it under the bleachers and rushed back to the school. I freshened my makeup as quickly as possible, brushed my hair to get out all the snarls the wind had blown into it, then ran back toward the bleachers.

It was as I ran back past the rear of the Roosevelt section that I noticed the new equipment stacked up there. *Roosevelt must have quite a show in store for us*, I thought. In addition to the megaphones they usually employed for their halftime shows, I saw rolled-up banners and fat, new-looking pom-poms stacked up, all in blue and burgundy, the Roosevelt school colors.

I also saw something that struck me as strange. Fooling around near the Roosevelt equipment was a scrawny kid about ten or eleven, and I almost said hello to him as I dashed by, sure it was Skeeter Watkins, Keith's little brother. Then my eyes fell on the burgundy-and-blue wool jacket he was wearing, and I closed my mouth. Of course it wasn't Keith's brother in a Roosevelt jacket. And I was in such a hurry to get back to the game that I didn't give it a second thought.

A few minutes later the Fieldcrest marching band took the field. No matter how many times I'd seen our band, I still felt the same fierce rush of pride as they marched on in two neat lines from opposite sides of the field, led by our high-stepping drum majors in plumed helmets, followed by short-skirted, baton-twirling majorettes. The color guard came from the center of our bleachers and met the others in midfield, each of the three guards bearing a different flag. One presented the Stars and Stripes, one a silvery Fieldcrest Falcon on a background of tan canvas, and one a flag with the word Welcome appliqued on it in many different languages. All in all, it was a stirring spectacle.

As the band went into formation, we took our places, half of us facing the Roosevelt side, half of us facing the home supporters. We didn't do regular cheers during the halftime show. This was our chance to show off our fancy footwork in carefully choreographed routines. In bigger schools most of the show was performed by a separate pom-pom squad, but at Fieldcrest we did it all.

And did we ever do it that day! We were fantastic as we rippled and kicked and did the high step in perfect unison. For one new routine, we all shook tambourines, and the cheerful jingling seemed to bounce back off the wooden bleachers. We did our last routine to resounding cheers and applause. I don't think a single Falcon fan was sitting at the end. Everyone was standing, stomping on the bleachers, and shouting their support.

Afterward there was a short break to give our band time to clear the field and the Roosevelt band time to group up. Because of the time of the year, it was beginning to grow dusky already, and the officials turned on the floodlights a little ahead of time so they wouldn't dazzle the Roosevelt performers in the middle of their show.

"Whew!" I exclaimed to April as we sank down in our section of the bleachers, still fighting for breath. "I'm glad we got to do our thing without those bright lights beating down on us. It may be a little cool today, but I sure worked up a sweat doing that last dance number. That's strenuous!"

"I'll bet it looked incredible from the stands," she said. "There's no way the Rattlers can come up with anything half as clever. Boy, if the Dallas Cowgirls had been here, even they'd be eating their hearts out!"

We were feeling great as we watched the Roosevelt band march onto the field. We were sure their entertainment couldn't live up to ours. Just as we had, their cheering squad jogged out single file to take their places—only, they were all facing the Fieldcrest side to start. Each of them carried a pom-pom in one hand and a giant megaphone in the other. Each megaphone had the cheerleader's name printed on it in bold letters.

"They must have some secret new routine, too," April muttered, suddenly sounding worried. "They've never come out with megaphones *and* pom-poms before."

"Ummm. Well, they can't have a more spectacular show than ours."

My eyes were glued to Mick, who was no more than fifty feet away from me, in the middle of the line of the Rattlers' cheerleaders. I remember thinking that he looked almost smug and that he'd probably never let me live it down if their routine was more professional than ours. Then my thoughts were drowned out by shock and horror as the cheerleaders lifted their megaphones to their lips.

In the hubbub and shouting and raucous, mocking laughter that followed, one thing was clear: we weren't going to get to see what Roosevelt had prepared for us. You see, someone had taken it upon himself or herself to prepare an even bigger surprise for the Rattler squad.

As Mick had raised his megaphone to his lips, he'd given a yell of startled fury. I watched in disbelief as red paint poured from the mouth of the megaphone, splattering all over his face and drenching his uniform. Mick didn't have a chance to jump out of the way. He just stood still as the rest of the squad gasped and the band's parade music ground to a halt.

After that, everything happened in rapid sequence. I saw Mrs. Schultz, our school nurse, rush onto the field to see if Mick had been hurt or even blinded by the paint, I guess. Then, surrounded by a surprised and concerned-looking group of Roosevelt cheerleaders, the two of them left the field with everyone headed toward the school building.

The next thing I knew, a voice was blaring over

the PA system, asking that people keep their seats. "The Roosevelt halftime show will not take place," the metallic voice of the announcer said solemnly, "but we expect the game to resume within fifteen minutes."

Following right on the heels of this, a voice that was easy to identify as our school principal's deep bass called the Falcon cheering squad to the girls' locker room "on the double."

We all jumped to our feet and started hurrying in that direction. None of it seemed real, and everyone on the squad seemed as stunned by what had happened as the Roosevelt kids were. I was rushing ahead of the others, terribly worried that Mick had been injured and desperate to make sure he was OK, when I remembered two things that suddenly assumed such importance I stumbled over my own feet and painfully went down on one knee.

Slowly I pushed myself up again, rubbing the spot that was grass-stained and raw. My head was spinning, and I felt ill. You see, I'd just recalled the premonition I'd had—as well as the sight of the little kid poking around the Rattlers' equipment and wearing a Roosevelt jacket!

Chapter Twelve

The Roosevelt squad—along with both school principals and Mrs. Schultz—was already in the locker room when we arrived. I saw immediately that Mick was missing, and my heart skipped a beat in terror. "Is he all right?" I asked.

None of the Rattlers would answer me. They just glared from the benches where they sat, their eyes dark with contempt. I almost yelled that *I* hadn't done anything. But on second thought I realized it was only natural for them to be disgusted with the whole bunch of us. After all, it was clearly someone from the Falcon side who'd pulled this cruel stunt.

"He's all right," Mrs. Schultz said in that calm way nurses always have. "Physically, that is. Though he'll be red and sore for a while after he finishes washing all that paint off his face.

"But he's fit to be tied, and I can't say I blame him. That wasn't a very funny prank. You should know better than to do something like that! You're too old not to realize someone could get hurt."

Naturally, there was a chorus of protests. It was clear that no one on the squad was going to admit to being involved in what had happened. Mr. Simmons, our principal, stepped forward from where he'd been talking to the principal from Roosevelt. "Mr. Hinman and I have discussed this, and I'm speaking for both of us when I say we have every intention of getting to the bottom of this appalling display of poor sportsmanship."

As a rule Mr. Simmons was a pretty long-winded guy, and from the way he stood ramrod straight—he'd been a naval officer and still acted as if he were addressing the troops—letting his gaze pass over each one of us in turn, I had a feeling he was warming up for a real lecture. But when Mick walked in—the back way, coming from the boys' locker room and showers—Mr. Simmons waited for him to get settled before going on. I guess he'd been an officer and a principal long enough to know that nobody was going to pay any attention to him until Mick's condition was checked out.

His uniform must have been totally ruined, so he'd changed into street clothes. Judging by what he had on—too-short corduroy jeans and a gray sweat shirt several sizes too large—I gathered he'd been told to take his pick from the lost and found. Even with most of the paint removed, Mick still looked awful. His face and neck were bright pink and looked sore from rubbing them.

Slumped on the bench, Mick looked up and smiled wanly at his squad mates as they reached over to squeeze his arm or slap him on the shoulder. He acted as if the Fieldcrest squad weren't in the room.

Clearing his throat, Mr. Simmons went on. "Both Mr. Hinman and I would like to see this football match played to the end. Of course, the game's already been ruined for Mick, but I'm sure he wouldn't want everyone else to suffer as well." Mick looked up then, long enough to nod in the general direction of Mr. Simmons, then he went back to staring at the floor.

"As principal of Fieldcrest, I would also like to see the Falcon cheerleaders cheering at every game until the end of the season. You're a squad I have always been proud of. However, I am willing to bet that the culprit is here in this room—or is known to someone here right now. I expect the Falcon cheerleaders to let me know who was responsible for this. In the past it's been the policy to overlook some of the harmless stunts you've pulled on each other, but this one went too far. It was unfunny and malicious."

Again he looked at us one by one, as if he were trying to determine if one of us had rigged Mick's megaphone. "You young people are cheer-leaders. You are supposed to represent the finest qualities of our school. Your fellow students look up to you. If one of you is guilty, I ask for a con-fession. If one of you knows the identity of our 'prankster,' I want the name. If, as you just pro-tested, you are all innocent, I want you to call upon your fellow students and ask them to urge whoever committed this act to come to me and admit it. Mr. Hinman and I will both be here dur-ing the entire third and fourth quarters of the game. That gives you all one full half to come to terms with my conditions. You see, there'll be no cheering from the Fieldcrest squad during the third and fourth quarters of this game."

I gasped along with the rest of the Falcon squad. No cheering for the most important half of the game! It didn't seem fair. It was terrible—but it got even worse a second later. "And if I'm not informed of the identity of the guilty party by the end of today's game, the entire Fieldcrest squad will be benched for the next three games."

"But that's not fair!" Will was brave enough to say what was on all our minds.

"Was what was done to Mick fair?" Mr.

Simmons asked. "I hate to be harsh, but if our cheering squad can't live up to the standards of fair play, honesty, good sportsmanship, and respect for their opponents, then they'll have to pay the price."

There was a long silence, and I knew Mr. Simmons was hoping someone would confess right away so we wouldn't have the threat of being benched hanging over our heads. I looked at Mick. He continued to stare at the floor, and my heart went out to him. He looked so miserable sitting there like that! I knew that to be singled out like that—and since all the Roosevelt megaphones had the cheerleader's name painted on the side, more than mere chance was involved in Mick's being the butt of the prank—had to be a blow to his ego and his pride. I wished whoever had done this to him would be brave enough to admit it so the whole ugly incident could be—

I bit my lip. Didn't I have a pretty good idea who was behind this whole thing? Everyone in town knew how Skeeter Watkins idolized Keith. Wouldn't he do whatever his big brother put him up to?

Just then Mick looked up, and our gazes locked. Nervously I looked away. Mick or no Mick, I had no intention of turning in Keith.

"Well, it seems no one's ready to tell me anything," Mr. Simmons said regretfully. "So let's go back to the game. Fieldcrest cheerleaders, you're not required to stay on the bench, but there will be no cheering. I hope to see one of you in here—for the sake of the whole squad."

As soon as it was clear we'd been dismissed, the Roosevelt squad surrounded Mick, everyone talking at once, voices raised in a mixture of sympathy and indignation. I saw my chance to slip away and joined the line of Falcons filing out the door with slumped shoulders and long faces. Now that I knew Mick was all right, I wanted to avoid him for a while. How could I feel at ease around him when I was pretty sure I knew who'd set up this attack on him?

I walked apart from the group. On the way back to the playing field with so much guilty knowledge churning inside me, how could I feel comfortable in anyone's company? Ahead of me, most of the Falcon squad members walked together, and I could hear them as they protested their innocence to one another. Keith, I noticed, was keeping unusually silent, which convinced me he was responsible for what had happened.

I was so lost in my muddled thoughts that I didn't hear Mick rush up behind me, and I wasn't aware of him at my heels until his voice rasped in my ear. "Where do you think you're going?"

"What's wrong?" I gasped, stunned at the bitterness in his voice. He'd never used a tone of voice like that with me before. "I mean, I know what's wrong, and it's a rotten thing to happen to anyone, but why are you glaring at me like that? Why are you acting like *I'm* to blame?" My voice broke.

"I don't think you did it," he said, his voice cold. "But I want you to tell me who did, Mandy."

"What makes you think I know?" I took a step backward, wishing I could keep going until I was far away.

"I can tell, that's all," he insisted. "The funny look that crossed your face when the principal was talking, the way you looked away from me like you were afraid I could read your mind, the guilty way you slipped out of the locker room just now." He laughed, a bitter, hollow sound. "Hey, maybe I was wrong, and you *did* do it yourself. Trying to put a little zing in our relationship, huh?"

"I don't think that's funny, Mick. You know I'd never do a mean thing like that. And I don't know who did."

"I don't believe you," he said simply. "I trust my intuition, and it tells me you know exactly who's behind this."

132

"I don't know!" I protested. Then honesty and the guilt of feeling like an unwilling accomplice won out, and I added, "Not for sure."

"Not for sure, huh?" His voice was sarcastic now. "Well, why don't you and I just go see Mr. Simmons and you call tell him who you *think* it might be?"

"What are you planning to do?" I asked, growing angry myself now. "Have some cheer-leader marched in front of Mr. Simmons and expelled or something just because I've got a *feeling* I know who's involved? That's crazy, Mick."

"Let me put it this way: I wouldn't expect a cheerleader to do a thing like that. Anyone's who's such a creep doesn't deserve to be on a squad. I wouldn't *want* to cheer next to someone who's got such a warped idea of fun. Do you?"

I took a deep breath, trying to remain calm. Beyond us, in the bleachers, I heard the buzzer signaling the start of the third quarter. "Listen, Mick, I know you're upset, and I don't blame you. But when you calm down, you'll see I'm right. I can't just turn in a fellow Falcon, certainly not one who could be innocent," I added, though the more I thought about it, the less I felt Keith was in the clear.

Now it was Mick who took a step away from me. He folded his arms across his chest, looking at me as if I were a total stranger—and not one he particularly wanted to get to know, either. "Is that all you have to say about this?"

Mick looked so forlorn standing there, it was all I could do not to fling my arms around him and tell him everything I knew. But then I'd be a traitor to my own side, and I knew that if Mick really cared for me, he'd never expect such a thing.

"I can't, Mick," I said, just about pleading with him. "I just can't turn in one of my own team-mates!"

"It's up to you, Mandy," Mick told me stiffly. "If you care more about protecting a Falcon than finding out who did this to me, that's your business. You're going to have to choose. I wouldn't have thought that was such a hard decision to make, but I guess I don't know you as well as I thought I did."

As Mick turned on his heel and stormed off in the direction of the Roosevelt stands, I had to fight back every instinct to call out to him. My eyes filled with tears as I stumbled along to join my squad.

Sitting on the bench along with the others, my mind was a whirl of confusion. Objectively, I knew that Mick was right. Rigging his mega-phone like that had been a terrible thing to do, and whoever was guilty deserved to be punished.

But for Mick to expect me to turn informer, to tell on a fellow squad member, was unfair. I just didn't know *what* was right or wrong anymore. And my only hope seemed to be that Keith would be decent enough to seek out Mr. Simmons on his own.

If he didn't, I'd be the biggest loser of all the people concerned. I'd lose my right to cheer for the next three games, and so would all the other Falcons. But I'd be the only one who'd lose my boyfriend as well.

Chapter Thirteen

For the next fifteen minutes or so, I watched Keith carefully. Maybe, I tried to tell myself, I'd made a mistake. Maybe it wasn't Skeeter Watkins I'd seen, after all. Maybe it was some Roosevelt kid wearing his own jacket and not doing anything wrong. But I'd have had to be blind not to notice that the usually laid-back and supercool Keith Watkins was behaving strangely.

Most of us were just slouching around pretending we were watching the game, though a few kids had gone off to talk to classmates, convinced the culprit wasn't someone on the squad and that they might be able to convince the guilty party to turn himself in. Keith did neither. He sat on the edge of the bleacher, turning around constantly as if looking for someone. I suspected he was keeping an eye out for his little brother so he could let him know they were in big trouble.

He caught me peering at him and made a big show of raising his eyebrows and shrugging his shoulders as if to say, "Isn't this terrible?" I made a little half shrug of my own, then looked away, pretending to be caught up in the action on the field. *How can you just sit there?* I wanted to ask Keith. *How can you let the rest of us pay for something we didn't do?* But I didn't say a word. I was afraid I'd make Keith even more defensive if I talked to him about the incident. As far as he knew, I was still Mick's girlfriend, so why should he trust me?

I don't know if it was Mick's absence from the line of Rattler cheerleaders or the fact that they felt strange leading cheers for their side when we couldn't cheer in return, but the zest had gone out of the Roosevelt squad. They chanted half-heartedly, their routines seemed lackluster, and their timing was off. I wondered if they cared, or even realized, that they were winning the game. Maybe the same thing was going on in their minds as in mine. Maybe they'd begun to realize we'd been so busy competing with each other as cheerleaders that we'd stopped caring about the players or the game. Mr. Simmons was right about poor sportsmanship. Only it wasn't just one person who'd been a bad sport—it was all of us, Roosevelt and Fieldcrest cheerleaders alike. Why, in the last few practice sessions, we hadn't even thought about keeping school spirit high. All we'd cared about was coming up with something extraspecial to make the Rattler squad look pathetic.

The buzzer signaling the end of the third quarter went off, and the Rattler squad straggled off the field for a rest. It was strangely quiet in the stands now. No doubt the fans were embarrassed for our squad, forced to sit there and not take part.

I felt that if I didn't walk off some of my nervous energy, I'd start screaming. So I jumped to my feet and grabbed my bag, deciding I'd go treat myself to a Coke and a candy bar. I'd have plenty of time for dieting during the dateless weekends to come.

April passed me on her way back to the bleachers as I was waiting in line. "Well, that's that," she said, sounding discouraged. "Everyone I talked to swears they don't know a thing. It looks like we'll be warming the benches for the next few weeks."

"Don't give up," I told her with more hope than I felt. "There's still a whole quarter to go."

But I was so nervous I ate the candy bar in three bites, barely tasting it. It was while I was standing there finishing my Coke that I realized

I had to do something. Seeing how depressed April had looked made me aware that I wasn't just hurting Mick by not taking steps to settle things with Keith—I was making the whole Fieldcrest squad pay for Keith's dirty trick.

But I couldn't simply turn him in. I realized then that the best way to handle the situation was to tell Keith face to face that I knew the truth and expected him to confess.

Feeling somewhat better now that I'd made a decision to take some kind of action, I went in search of Keith. I didn't even make it back to the stands before I saw him. He was standing away from the crowd, talking seriously to his brother, Skeeter, who wasn't wearing a Roosevelt jacket this time around.

"Keith!" I called. "Come here a sec, would you?"

Keith said something else to Skeeter, who hurried away, then he headed over toward me. My stomach was in knots as I prepared to face an awkward, ugly scene.

"Keith, it's about—" I began.

"Look, Mandy, I can't talk now." He sounded tense and angry. "I've got something to take care of."

"But this is important," I protested. "You see—"

He interrupted me again. "Whatever it is, it

can't be more important than my seeing Mr. Simmons and straightening everything out."

"What? You're going to tell him you put Skeeter up to it?"

"Put Skeeter up to it?" Keith's voice cracked, then he laughed, and when he spoke again, he seemed less tense. "What happened, Mandy, did you see Skeeter doing something and think I was the brains behind it? Hey, my sense of humor's not *that* demented!"

I shook my head. "I don't understand."

He sighed impatiently, then said lightly, "Well, I guess you deserve an explanation, seeing how you obviously knew something was up and didn't tell on me. In a way, I guess I did put Skeeter up to it. Only, I didn't know it. See, last night I was pretty fed up with Mick Farris—for acting like such a creep when all I'd done was tried to make a joke out of his accusing you of stealing his routine. So I made the mistake of saying something to Skeeter about how I'd heard through a friend at Roosevelt that their cheerleaders were going to do a megaphone routine and I had half a mind to booby-trap Mick's megaphone with a water balloon."

"You mean that's all you said?"

Keith had the good grace to look embarrassed. "Well, to tell the truth, I went a little further. See, Skeeter said he bet I was making the whole thing up and that something like that was impossible to do. So, just to show off and impress the kid, I got out a balloon and some thread and showed him how it's done—without a megaphone, of course."

"How *is* it done?"

"It's sort of complicated, but basically you fill a balloon with water and tie it loosely with a piece of thread. Then you run the thread through the mouthpiece and tie it around the outside of the rim—carefully, so it can't be noticed. You take the other end of the thread and tape it along the inside of the megaphone near the big end to hold the balloon in place, with the balloon taped along the inside, too. As soon as the mega-phone's raised up at a sharp angle, all the water rushes out."

"But it wasn't water—it was paint! And Skeeter had on a Roosevelt jacket."

"What can I tell you?" He shrugged. "The kid got smart and improvised. I mean, he *is* just a kid, and when he spotted a half-empty paint can in the garage this morning, he decided paint would be ever better than water. And he just happened to 'borrow' a Rattlers jacket he saw lying in someone's unlocked car. Figured he'd be safer behind enemy lines that way." He laughed. "That's what he just finished telling me, anyway. You see, as soon as it happened, I put two and two together. But I didn't want to talk to Mr. Simmons until I'd actually found Skeeter and gotten the truth from him. I expected him to come to me, but the poor kid's terrified. I think he's afraid Mr. Simmons is going to throw him in jail!"

"Boy, am I glad it's all getting straightened out!" I said thankfully.

"Me, too," Keith agreed. "Now I'd better head for the locker room. I sure learned one thing: the next time I'll think twice before I go shooting my mouth off in front of Skeeter."

He jogged off, and I headed back to my seat. I was glad Keith hadn't done a rotten thing like that on purpose, and I could understand Skeeter's not realizing the seriousness of his prank. Mr. Simmons might be stern, but I couldn't believe he'd punish Keith for something his kid brother did, and in spite of Skeeter's fears, I knew he wasn't going to get too harsh a punishment. So if everything was all right, I thought, why did I still feel like crying?

There were five minutes left in the last quarter, but only a miracle could help Fieldcrest win the game now. I stood up, and as I brushed past Bev, I told her I was going to the ladies' room. Soon she and the other kids would learn what I already knew: that the booby trap hadn't been set by anyone on the squad and we weren't going to be benched. By then, I'd be halfway home. I couldn't see any reason for staying until the end because I realized that Keith's giving a full explanation to Mr. Simmons really didn't have much bearing on the flare-up between Mick and me.

Mick had made it clear, for once and for all, that he expected my first loyalty to be to him and not to my school. If I'd turned in Keith or if I'd at least been willing to let Mick in on my suspicions, he'd have been satisfied. Then and only then.

This showed that Mick and I had completely different ideas about loyalty. And about love. I didn't see how things could ever work out between us. So I was just going to have to give up Mick.

That's why I left the game and started walking home. I didn't see how Keith's telling the truth about what had happened could change things for Mick and me, and I had no desire to hang around and listen to Mick gripe about Keith's having it in for him.

I'd almost made it to the house when I was surprised by Mick's familiar old heap pulling up at the curb beside me. He turned off the lights and ignition and rolled down his window. "You left," he said. "I went over to the Fieldcrest stands to look for you, and Bev said you'd never come back from the girls' room."

"I wasn't in the girls' room." I stopped walking but stayed where I was on the sidewalk. "I didn't see any reason for sticking around. There wasn't a prayer that the Falcons might win."

"Roosevelt won by twenty points," he said, not sounding as smug as I'd thought he would. "But why didn't you wait?"

"I already told you."

"But if you'd waited, you'd know that everything's all right, Mandy!"

"You mean about Keith's brother rigging your megaphone?" I shook my head. "I was looking for Keith to tell him I couldn't keep my mouth shut about seeing Skeeter. I ran into him on his way to see Mr. Simmons."

"What do you mean? Don't you want to know what happened when he came to the locker room?"

"You mean, don't I want to hear you gloat over Keith's having to admit to the principal that his brother never would have done something like that if he hadn't put the idea in his head? The answer's no, Mick. I like Keith, and I don't feel like listening to you put him down and go on about how he's always had it in for you. And, in case you've forgotten," I reminded him pointedly, "I didn't make the choice you gave me in your ultimatum. I didn't choose squealing over loyalty to my school and the rest of my friends!"

"You've got it all wrong, Mandy. Hey, I know I said stuff I shouldn't have, but I was still in shock then. You really do have it all wrong," he repeated. "Come on, please! Get in the car and let me explain what really happened. Don't you think you owe me that much?"

"All right," I said reluctantly, going around to the passenger side. I closed the door behind me, then leaned against it facing Mick. "What really happened?"

"Well, I'd cooled off and gone back down to the locker room to talk to Mr. Simmons and Mr. Hinman. The more I thought about it, the more it didn't seem right for everyone on your squad to be punished for something done by a single person. The whole thing was starting to make me feel as if I were the bad guy and not the victim. And as far as I could see, your principal's coming down on the whole squad because of what happened was just going to make things that much tougher between Roosevelt and Fieldcrest."

"I never thought it was fair to threaten everyone," I put in.

"According to Mr. Simmons, he didn't, either. But he thought that might be the only way to get whoever had done it to tell the truth."

"Were you there when Keith came in?" I asked, not bothering to hide my curiosity now.

He nodded. "After everything was said and done, Mr. Simmons admitted it wasn't fair to punish Keith for something he'd set in motion without meaning to. And I guess poor Skeeter's been punished enough for trying to help his brother. Keith said the kid was terrified."

"And you really don't care that Keith didn't get into trouble?"

"Of course not," Mick assured me. "The whole thing wasn't really his fault. And to tell you the truth, once Keith and I started talking, I realized what a great guy he is. We both saw that we'd been letting the competition get out of hand. I guess what happened today made us both realize how terrible we'd feel if our attitudes were to blame for the rivalry not being fun anymore. It's all grown too serious."

"We sure forgot all the stuff we learned in camp in a hurry, didn't we?" I remarked. "All those ideals about 'may the best man win' and the spirit of brotherhood. We're all responsible for turning the rivalry into a full-fledged battle."

"Yeah," Mick agreed slowly, "but I'm the only one responsible for trying to get you to turn in one of your squad mates. I know I'd never tell on a friend, so what right did I have to expect you to do it?"

"You do understand then. You see that I couldn't tell you about Keith? I didn't know for sure that he was responsible, anyhow. I just spotted a kid who looked like Skeeter hanging around in a Roosevelt jacket, and put two and two together later."

"Of course I understand," Mick said warmly. "I'd never forgive myself if I'd pushed you into doing something you thought was wrong. I had no right to force you to choose."

"Oh, why does everything have to be such a mess?" I wailed. "Now I'm afraid it was our personal competitiveness that rubbed off on the other cheerleaders and made them worse. Maybe I just can't compete against you as a cheerleader and be your girlfriend, too."

"Don't say that, Mandy!" He slid an arm around my shoulders and pulled me away from the door, closer to him. "Don't you see? We never should have been competing with each other in the first place. That's not our role. A cheerleader's job is to lead the cheers, and that's all. We're not supposed to be trying to look better than the kids on the other school's squad. It's the players who are supposed to be competing. And maybe Troy isn't so wrong about competition not always being such a hot thing."

"Oh, I hope you're right," I said with feeling. "There's nothing I want more than for cheerleading to be fun again, and for you and me to be proud of each other. I just hope the other kids feel the same way."

"We'll just have to convince them," Mick murmured, tilting my chin up. "We'll have to show everyone just how beautifully Roosevelt and Fieldcrest can get along—if they really try."

We didn't do much talking after that. You might say we were too busy proving what a great combination Roosevelt and Fieldcrest were together—in the kissing department, at least!

Epilogue

That all happened last year, and I think it's only fair of me to let you know what happened afterward.

At school the next Monday, one person after another came up to me to tell me what a great guy Mick was. You see, what Mick hadn't bothered telling me was that Mr. Simmons was considering kicking Keith off the squad in spite of everything, worried the administration would look weak if someone wasn't made to pay. Mick had convinced the principal that he shouldn't hold Keith responsible.

So I suppose Keith's dopey kid brother helped us in a roundabout way by stopping our warfare before it really got out of hand.

Mick graduated in June, and now I go to all the Yale games with him. We're still going together. And would you believe neither Roosevelt nor Fieldcrest won the championship? Some dinky little school none of us had ever taken seriously sneaked up from behind and outclassed everyone!

Keith and Bev are seeing each other now, and both of them are on the Fieldcrest squad with me again this year. It's hard to believe we all survived to be seniors.

Joy Moran got kicked out of Harrisville in a big cheating scandal. Now she's going to private school, the same one her cousin goes to. Yes, Ricki convinced her folks the reason she wasn't popular at Fieldcrest was that we were all so "common." She didn't even finish out the year before transferring back to her boarding school.

I heard from Danny. One measly postcard.

Carla's on the squad this year. She didn't take it too hard when she and Keith started drifting apart in the spring. Like I said, Carla was always known for being fickle. But she's changed since she started going out with Troy. He's at Yale with Mick now, and the four of us double-date a lot. It looks as if Carla's finally found her romantic ideal. She's also five dollars richer, having finally made me pay off the bet I lost to her.

Real and Joanna are *still* an item. Only, now they're just Reid and Jo. "Everyone's calling themselves such weird names these days, it's more exotic just to be someone simple," she told me after coming to her senses. Capital Punishment changed its name to Death Row Pardon, which is a step in the right direction, if not a vast improvement.

Oh, yeah. Germany was terrific. I loved the food and the people and the customs and the Black Forest so much, I hardly even minded not seeing Mick for two weeks. I wrote to him every day, though.

While I was in Germany, I sent a postcard to Danny. I wanted to let him know I got around.

Sweet Dreams ®

We hope you enjoyed reading this book. All the titles currently available in the Sweet Dreams series are listed on the next two pages. Ask for them in your local bookshop or newsagent. Two new titles are published each month.

If you would like to know more about Sweet Dreams, or if you have difficulty obtaining any of the books locally, or if you would like to tell us what you think of the series, write to:—

<table>
<tr><td>

United Kingdom
Kim Prior,
Corgi Books,
Century House,
61-63 Uxbridge Road,
London W5 5SA,
England

</td><td>

Australia
Sally Porter,
Corgi and
Bantam Books,
26 Harley Crescent,
Condell Park 220,
N.S.W., Australia

</td></tr>
</table>

17850 4	THE TRUTH ABOUT ME AND BOBBY V (41)	Janetta Johns
17851 2	THE PERFECT MATCH (42)	Marian Woodruff
17850 2	TENDER LOVING CARE (43)	Anne Park
17853 9	LONG DISTANCE LOVE (44)	Jesse Dukore
17069 4	DREAM PROM (45)	Margaret Burman
17070 8	ON THIN ICE (46)	Jocelyn Saal
17071 6	TE AMO MEANS I LOVE YOU (47)	Deborah Kent
17072 4	DIAL L FOR LOVE (48)	Marian Woodruff
17073 2	TOO MUCH TO LOSE (49)	Suzanne Rand
17074 0	LIGHTS, CAMERA, LOVE (50)	Gailanne Maravel
17075 9	MAGIC MOMENTS (51)	Debra Spector
17076 7	LOVE NOTES (52)	Joanna Campbell
17087 2	GHOST OF A CHANCE (53)	Janet Quin-Harkin
17088 0	I CAN'T FORGET YOU (54)	Lois I. Fisher
17089 9	SPOTLIGHT ON LOVE (55)	Nancy Pines
17090 2	CAMPFIRE NIGHTS (56)	Dale Cowan
17871 7	ON HER OWN (57)	Suzanne Rand
17872 5	RHYTHM OF LOVE (58)	Stephanie Foster
17873 3	PLEASE SAY YES (59)	Alice Owen Crawford
17874 1	SUMMER BREEZES (60)	Susan Blake
17875 X	EXCHANGE OF HEARTS (61)	Janet Quin-Harkin
17876 8	JUST LIKE THE MOVIES (62)	Suzanne Rand
24150 8	KISS ME, CREEP (63)	Marian Woodruff
24151 6	LOVE IN THE FAST LANE (64)	Rosemary Vernon
24152 4	THE TWO OF US (65)	Janet Quin-Harkin
24153 2	LOVE TIMES TWO (66)	Stephanie Foster
24180 X	I BELIEVE IN YOU (67)	Barbara Conklin
24181 8	LOVEBIRDS (68)	Janet Quin-Harkin
24254 7	CALL ME BEAUTIFUL (69)	Shannon Blair
24255 5	SPECIAL SOMEONE (70)	Terri Fields
24355 1	TOO MANY BOYS (71)	Celia Dickenson
24356 X	GOODBYE FOREVER (72)	Barbara Conklin
24357 8	LANGUAGE OF LOVE (73)	Rosemary Vernon
24381 0	DON'T FORGET ME (74)	Diana Gregory
24382 9	FIRST SUMMER LOVE (75)	Stephanie Foster

NON-FICTION TITLES

17859 8	THE SWEET DREAMS BEAUTIFUL HAIR BOOK	Courtney DeWitt
17838 5	THE LOVE BOOK	Deidre Laiken and Alan Schneider
17845 8	THE BODY BOOK	Deidre Laiken and Alan Schneider
17077 5	HOW TO TALK TO BOYS AND OTHER IMPORTANT PEOPLE	Catherine Winters